Hugh Reginald Haweis

American Humorists

outlook

Hugh Reginald Haweis

American Humorists

Reprint of the original, first published in 1883.

1st Edition 2024 | ISBN: 978-3-38532-980-5

Verlag (Publisher): Outlook Verlag GmbH, Zeilweg 44, 60439 Frankfurt, Deutschland
Vertretungsberechtigt (Authorized to represent): E. Roepke, Zeilweg 44, 60439 Frankfurt, Deutschland
Druck (Print): Books on Demand GmbH, In de Tarpen 42, 22848 Norderstedt, Deutschland

AMERICAN HUMORISTS

LECTURES DELIVERED AT THE
ROYAL INSTITUTION

BY THE

Rev. H. R. HAWEIS, M.A.

AUTHOR OF "MUSIC AND MORALS," "THOUGHTS FOR THE TIMES,"
"CURRENT COIN," "ARROWS IN THE AIR," ETC.

SECOND EDITION

—London

CHATTO AND WINDUS, PICCADILLY

1883

PROLOGUE.

IN reprinting these Lectures, the first four of which I delivered at the Royal Institution last year (1881), I am quite aware that what was spoken extemporaneously, and intended originally only to be *heard* in a genial atmosphere, must lose some of its effect when *read* in cold blood.

But the numerous imperfect shorthand reports which appeared, not only upon the first delivery of my "AMERICAN HUMORISTS" at the Royal Institution, but also after their repetition at the London Institution in the spring of the present year (1882), convinced me that nothing worse could happen to them, even were I to throw my own notes together and print them in a volume.

I have done so, and can at least plead Thackeray's example in my favour.

Thackeray's " ENGLISH HUMORISTS " were first heard in the lecture-room.

I can only hope that the " Wit and Wisdom " of others in the following pages will be found, if not enhanced, at least not impaired by the setting which I have here supplied, and which so lately appeared to receive the hearty approval of " crowded houses," both in the east and west of London.

I may add that the Dandelion on the cover (*dent de lion*), despoiled of the six floating seeds —one symbolic seed for each of my Humorists —appeared to me to indicate aptly enough the incisive bite, yet vagrant character, of Wit.

Wit often seizes its prey with a truly leonine grip; yet sometimes it has to wander far in search of an appropriate soil,—in vain do its seedlets fall upon minds without a sense of humour.

For the fate of these seeds which have been blown across the Atlantic I have no fear. They have long since taken root; and a glance at the full Dandelion ball that remains is enough to show that plenty more are ready to take wing from the same quarter, and to find, let us hope, a pleasant resting-place upon British soil.

H. R. HAWEIS.

LONDON,
October, 1882.

CONTENTS.

I.

WASHINGTON IRVING.

AMERICAN HUMORISTS.

I.

WASHINGTON IRVING.

FOREWORDS ON HUMOUR AND WIT.

 FEW words on wit and humour in general; a few more on American wit and humour in particular; and a good many on the wit and humour of WASHINGTON IRVING, OLIVER WENDELL HOLMES, JAMES RUSSELL LOWELL, ARTEMUS WARD, MARK TWAIN, and BRET HARTE.

I have read long and tiresome essays by HAZLITT and others, explaining the difference between wit and humour.

I have lain awake at night thinking over the difference, and I have come to the conclusion—that there is none.

I hasten to reveal this truth to the world because it has been such a comfort to me.

Humour is the electric atmosphere, wit is the flash. A situation provides the atmospheric humour, and with the culminating point of it comes the flash.

The character of CARLYLE's " Teufelsdroeckh " is perfectly steeped in a peculiar kind of dry and flowing humour, but

when he says that England is composed of ten million of
human beings—*mostly fools*, there is the flash.   Out of such
a tone of mind from such a humorous atmosphere, we may
expect to draw a spark at almost any moment.

COWPER's "John Gilpin" provides a series of situations
from which we naturally have great expectations; and, in
fact, at each turning-point there comes the inevitable flash
of wit proper to the humorous situation.   As the worthy
citizen flies helplessly past the place where he should have
dined—

> " ' Stop, stop, John Gilpin !—Here's the house !
>   They all at once did cry ;
>   ' The dinner waits, and we are tired : '
>   Said Gilpin, ' *So am I!* ' "

" a hit—a palpable hit ! "

There are some people who turn away from such light
themes.   They consider fun dangerous, humour frivolous,
wit waste of time.   They are wrong.

I assert the dignity of wit, and I claim for it noble ends,
for, rightly used, it is sensible, moral, recreative, and stimulating in a very high degree.

PORSON said, "Wit is the best sense in the world." Everything truly witty is a very nucleus of condensed thought—a
sort of literary Liebig, an "extractum carnis" of sense.

Analyze any "good saying" or "*bon mot*," you will find
it will bear sifting—thinking about, and will generally rivet
upon the mind something worth remembering.

A conceited poet once asked PORSON to read a new
poem which he had just written, and tell him candidly what
he thought of it.   "Sir," said the great scholar, "your
verse will be read when VIRGIL is forgotten, *but not till
then !* "   Was there no *sense* in that ?

"Doctor, how do you live to be so old and rich ? "   "By

writing prescriptions, but never taking them," was the witty and very *sensible* reply.

"Man," says a proverb, "leads woman to the altar, and there his leadership ends." This is a truth which has doubtless been so often and so happily illustrated in the lives and experiences of the people whom I have the honour of addressing, that I need hardly do more than allude to it here.

I need not go far afield to prove that wit is a moral force.

No one will deny that Mr. SPURGEON'S wit has a great deal to do with his vast ministerial success, and that he has used it on the whole wisely and well. Indeed, there have been few great preachers who have not made trenchant use of wit and satire.

The great Reformation orators, not to speak of Cromwell's preachers, were notorious humorists.

The modern French preachers, the Irish, and most of the Italians, especially in the south, are not deficient in pulpit humour—nor afraid to use it either.

One wet Sunday, ROWLAND HILL, noticing some people who had taken refuge inside his chapel from the rain, remarked, "I have heard of people making a cloak of their religion, but this is the first time I have ever known them make an umbrella of it."

Indeed, a stroke of humour from the pulpit will not only arrest, but will often impress when even impassioned oratory would fall flat.

If you cannot make men ashamed of doing wrong, you may often make them afraid of being ridiculous.

A man who does not feel that he is sinful, may often be convinced that he is absurd.

But wit is not only highly moral, but extremely recreative and stimulating.

The mind goes round normally one way, wit turns it round the other ; the very process is refreshing.

An old horse, who six days in the week was driven round and round in a lime-kiln, was left to himself on Sunday, and how do you suppose he rested ? It was observed that at a certain hour—corresponding to the time when he was usually put into harness—he got up and went round the other way. This set up a reverse action in his brain, and refreshed him.

We all require to unwind ourselves, and wit is one of the most powerful unwinders.

Let me analyze wit. It always involves an exaggeration, a reversal of ideas, a glimpse of the incongruous or the impossible.

When in dreams you see a mouse as big as a house, you are not surprised or amused, because in sleep you lose your sense of comparison ; but a mouse as big as a house, or a blue-bottle as big as an ox, in a pantomime is a certain success.

When the clown stands admiringly to watch the horses put through their ingenious paces by the flash groom with the long whip, and at last, after carefully ogling the quadrupeds, remarks to the audience, "It is astonishing what you can learn insects," the reversal of ideas is recreative, and our delight is genuine at suddenly finding a horse alluded to as a gnat or a moth.

When DICKENS tells us of a lady who was carried home in a "flood of tears and a sedan chair," we are all pleasantly affected by an immediate sense of the incongruous.

When the proverbial showman produces a small skull, and assures the company that it is "the real skull of the poet BURNS *when* he was a little boy," the shock of the impossible falls upon us like a cold shower-bath. When he further exhibits a stuffed crocodile, and remarks, "This hexentric animal, ladies and gentlemen, in'abits a desert island seventy-five miles removed from either land or water," the very naturalness of the sound makes the outrageous nonsense all the more agreeable.

Now to sum up : Humour is the atmosphere, wit the flash.

Humour lies in the situation, wit in its culminating points.

It is sensible, moral, recreative, and stimulating.

It always involves a shock of some kind, either of exaggeration, reversal of ideas, a sense of the incongruous or impossible.

Its dignity is vindicated, its nature analyzed.

American wit has three main roots.

These roots seem part and parcel of the national character, and are inseparably connected with the early history of our American cousins.

First, I notice the shock between Business and Piety. That is always a fruitful source of comedy to outsiders. Those famous Pilgrim Fathers who went over in the *Mayflower*, to create a new civilization and conquer a new world, were singularly wide awake as well as pious. They were martyrs to a religious idea, but they were keenly alive to the practical interests of real life.

I have nothing to say against religion and business going hand in hand. The two occupy parallel but not necessarily antagonistic planes, and have, or ought to have, frequent side-channels of communication; but the habits and instincts developed by each are too often practically irreconcilable, and sometimes flagrantly inconsistent.

" John," said the pious grocer, " have you sanded the

sugar?" "Yes, sir." "Larded the butter?" "Yes, sir." "Floured the ginger?" "Yes, sir." "Then come in to prayers."

The brisk competition between business and piety, together with the various cross lines of thought and feeling which it begets—derived no doubt from the thrift and 'cuteness of the early settlers—underlies a good deal of the modern American wit.

The Pilgrims were far too grim and grave to joke; but their descendants, who are fully alive to their peculiarities and weaknesses, whilst inheriting a full share of both, are not so particular.

WASHINGTON IRVING's skit on the Yankee lawyer who became a converted man upon seeing a ghost, and after that never cheated—"except when it was to his own ad- vantage," is a fair thrust at that spirit which has the "form of godliness, denying the power thereof," and which, however morally deplorable, has an irresistibly comic side to it.

Another deep undertone of American humour is the forcible and national contrast for ever present to the American mind between the Yankee and the poor Red Man whom he has supplanted.

WASHINGTON IRVING and ARTEMUS WARD have both made great play with this element. The picture in "Knicker- bocker" of the wily Dutch trader sitting down opposite the red man, and smoking gravely with him "the calumet of peace," listening to the poetical savage's interminable tirades of oratory *à la* FENIMORE COOPER, and puffing away gravely without understanding a word of it, but never omitting to put in a "Yah! mein Herr!" at each pause, with a stolid and Batavian gravity—that is a feature quite peculiar to and inseparable from the national life and humour.

Lastly, the contrast between the vastness of American nature and the smallness of man, especially European man, seems to be a never-failing source of amusement to Yankee humorists.

Their general ability to "whip creation" turns largely upon the bigness of their rivers, mountains, and prairies, and the superior enterprise generated by these immensities.

By one wit, Niagara is valued because it could put out "our" Vesuvius in "ten minutes." Our biggest rivers are. to the Mississippi and Missouri as babbling streams, our lakes are mere ponds; even the Alps and Pyrenees begin to look puny; and as to fields and woods, they are as paddocks and shrubberies to the virgin forests and boundless prairies of yon mighty Transatlantic continent.

The American visitor who was asked how he liked the Isle of Wight, is said to have replied, "It was well enough, but so dangerous;" and when asked to explain, he said the fact was the island was so small that when he got out of bed in the morning, he found himself in danger of tumbling into the sea!

To sum up the peculiarities of American humour:

First, there is the shock between Business and Piety.

Secondly, the shock of contrast between the Aboriginal and the Yankee.

Lastly, the shock of contrast between the bigness of American nature and the smallness of European nature, or, as for the matter of that, Human Nature itself outside America.

You will notice that I have only selected a certain number of Amerian humorists; and when I published my list, people at the Royal Institution asked me, "Why do you omit JAMES, and CABLE, and LELAND, and HOWELLS, and so forth?"

I have noticed in life that whenever a man sets himself to do one thing, his friends always ask him why he did not do something else.

In this case my reply was—

"I select those men, without prejudice to any others, who in my opinion suffice to embody the genius of American humour, as far as it has got."

Then I was asked—

"Why begin with WASHINGTON IRVING?"

"Simply because WASHINGTON IRVING was the first considerable American writer."

"But why call him a humorist?"

"Because he *was* a humorist. He was a great deal more, but he was *that*. SHAKESPEARE and SCOTT were a great deal more, but they were humorists. I might deal with IRVING as an historian or a biographer or an essayist, but I leave these varied and important aspects on one side in order to deal with him as a humorist—the first humorist, the father of American humour."

I should now like WASHINGTON IRVING to step out of the historical canvas and salute you in person, before I dwell upon his characteristics,—the flashes of his wit, the atmosphere of his humour.

I like to dwell upon that genial, modest, quiet gentleman, roused only at times into bursts of overflowing fun; but often rippling on with a pleasant provocative humour, a ready sparkle, a quiet repartee, yet prone, too prone, to hide his light under a bushel, giving his best things out only to his best friends, and averse to all show or flattery, and even half averse to fame.

There never was any one who so carried the whole of

himself in each of his writings. The charm of that personal wit and simplicity of character, not without a certain playful subtlety, is never absent.

He seldom rises or falls. He is neither more nor less than himself, and *that* is always delightful, sincere, thorough, and buoyant.

WASHINGTON IRVING was born on April 3, 1783, at New York. He died in 1859. His mother was English; his father was Scotch. He was named after WASHINGTON. He was once in a shop with his nurse, when WASHINGTON came in. The great patriot patted the little fellow on the head, and IRVING'S connection with the saviour of his country began and ended there.

In school hours he feasted on travels and tales, and hated arithmetic.

It is a remarkable and consoling fact that many great men have hated arithmetic. They have had many followers who have resembled them in nothing else.

His health as a boy was not good, and he was sent on a voyage up the Hudson river. Judge KENT, who heard him coughing, remarked, he "was evidently not long for this world."

He put up at an inn, which seems to have been far from an ideal hostelry, as he left the following affecting lines written up over the mantelpiece :—

" Here sovereign Dirt erects her sable throne,
The house, the host, the hostess all her own."

In 1804 he sails for Europe, coughing as usual. The captain remarked, "That chap will go overboard."

Having thus been twice killed by sympathetic strangers, he has the good fortune to be boarded by a privateer on the voyage, and the further luck to fall in with Admiral NELSON'S fleet in the Mediterranean.

He hurries through Rome to London, catches a glimpse of the SIDDONS, and another of KEMBLE ; and after some desultory attempts to write, in conjunction with his brother Peter, we find him back in New York in 1809, the publication date, by the way, of his famous "Knickerbocker Papers"—a little fact which perhaps explains the singular indulgence with which he was treated by his elder brothers, who had gone into business.

Like other men of talent, IRVING took to the law, but the law did not take to him.

He took also to the daughter of his law-coach, who took to him, but died at the age of eighteen.

Was that his first, last love ? The world is always curious about these things. "Tôt ou tard tout se sçait," says a French proverb. But the love-secrets of some men will never be known ; IRVING may be one of those men.

Perhaps IRVING had no secrets ; perhaps he had. A little sentiment leaks out here and there—a hint, a surmise, a possibility, perhaps a disappointment.

He certainly was attached to the Foster family. He was an *enfant de la maison* there ; perhaps some of us know what that means.

The regard, friendship, admiration, and love of tender, gracious women ; the culture, the repose, the relaxation, and sweetness of their society. The atmosphere in which passion might wake, but does not wake ; where life and thought and feeling are quickened, heightened by the full, fervent, and exhilarating atmosphere of mutual appreciation, the companionship of true hearts, the happy ebb and flow of genial spirits !

Yet with Emily Foster, it seems, there was something more than this ; something which might have ripened into love—which perhaps did so ripen. I find, here and there, allusions to starlight whispers, long walks in the mountains, terrible carriage accidents in Alpine ravines. I find the young people leaning over balconies together on summer nights. I read of long evenings, and tea and music and quiet chats in cosy nooks.

But, for various reasons, we are given to understand that marriage was not contemplated, one reason being that Emily married another.

There was some pain about all this; the shadow of loss was over it—the weariness of separation, and that sad bowing to the inevitable which sometimes leaves a scar which all the mellowing influence of the reconciling years cannot wholly efface. But I anticipate.

IRVING'S attempts to get into harness turn out failures. Evidently the law won't do, and his brothers propose, with some diffidence, a little commercial arithmetic at the desk.

To IRVING'S honour be it said that he never absolutely shirked this. He actually went through it, resignedly enough at times on a pinch; but his kinsfolk had the wit to trust his literary instincts, and so he appears before us at the age of twenty-nine, in 1812, as a gentleman of leisure, fond of society, much courted as a witty and genial friend, making a good figure in drawing-rooms, fond of travelling about, dallying at times with business which he never really understood, and looking after appointments which he never got.

IRVING took to England as a duck takes to the water.

He seems never happier than when getting together the elements of "Bracebridge Hall," which may be called the coronation of English country life.

Something in our fields and woods, and village pastimes, and old manorial residences, with their old semi-despotic patriarchal ways of quaint hospitality and simple heartiness, even the ignorance and narrowness of provincial life, would

be lighted up with flashes of wit and sly side-thrusts of no
unfriendly satire.

And his touch is always light, yet firm and adequate.
The Squire, Master Simon, Christy, the Housekeeper, are
really alive, because thoroughly felt with the heart as well
as seen with the eye.

Like some thorough Americans who are eager not to be
mistaken for Englishmen, IRVING loved Englishmen.   He
liked our ways, he adored our ruins, he reverenced our
traditions; and though a regular republican, if indeed he
was a regular anything in politics, he swallowed the British
constitution whole, and thought it quite right—for England.

He associated naturally with our foremost men of letters,
and what men we had then!   The world was still talking
about PORSON, BURKE, HORNE-TOOKE, who had but
recently passed away.   ROGERS had known them, and in
London society one got the everyday chat of men like
BYRON, the DUKE OF WELLINGTON, WALTER SCOTT, MOORE,
COLERIDGE, SOUTHEY, LAMB; and later on, DICKENS,
BULWER, HARRISON AINSWORTH, TENNYSON, and BROWN-
ING.

He delighted in old ROGERS, at whose famous breakfasts
he met the author of "Waverley," obliging enough to tell
him that he was like SWIFT and STERNE; JEFFREY, that
critical swashbuckler, that Leo Fulvus, who for his good
friend IRVING would hide his fierce claw, and "roar as gentle
as a sucking dove" over "Knickerbocker" in the *Edinburgh
Review;* TOM MOORE, who patted him on the back, laughed
at him for shutting up in mixed company, and said he was
"not strong as a lion, but delightful as a domestic animal;"
Mrs. SIDDONS, who read his works with emotion, and remarked twice when she met him, and each time with her
grand tragedy air, "Mr. IRVING, you made me cry!"

IRVING was a free lance in literature; anything like business bored him.

He was delightfully desultory, and yet capable of sustained effort, as in his life of WASHINGTON or COLUMBUS, where his heart went with the work.

When he wrote merely for money, as in the life of MAHOMET, he crammed conscientiously, and was simply dull.

He hated magazine-editing, and loved magazine-writing.

Full of amiable inconsistency, he disliked politics, yet lived to be Secretary of Legation at London and Ambassador at Madrid.

If anything, he was a republican, yet had an excessive admiration for NAPOLEON BONAPARTE.

He respected the English monarchy, but described GEORGE IV. as a bloated sensualist, and a mere "inflation of sack and sugar," which must have gratified the gentle soul of THACKERAY.

In 1818 the firm of IRVING BROTHERS failed, and we find brother WASHINGTON, who had little to do with the firm or the failure, characteristically refusing a good Government appointment, and buckling to, manfully, pen in hand, to make both ends meet.

In 1819 he offers MURRAY the publisher his famous "Sketch-book," which, owing perhaps to a strong recommendation from WALTER SCOTT, is all the more eagerly accepted. Soon afterwards he leaves London for Paris, Aix, and Wiesbaden.

His health seems indifferent; but, it must be added, he appears at this time—he was thirty-six—rather indifferent to his health. He complains of inability to write, but under the circumstances that was not surprising.

"I am writing with a bewildered head and feverish hand, having *returned at almost daylight from a fancy ball at the British Ambassador's.*"

Many people have felt like IRVING under similar circumstances, who have not resembled him in much else.

The fact is, his books, which were the first of their kind —the "roundabout kind"—were by this time a good deal read, and IRVING was a good deal courted in polite society.

His genial modesty, his kindly heart, his honourable life and gentle manners, endeared him to a large circle of friends; whilst his delicate humour, never quite at command or under control, often made him a charming companion.

LONGFELLOW speaks of his "playful wit," "his sunny temperament," and "his open heart."

But he was soon chilled, and easily depressed, though apt to recover himself rapidly.

He was very sensitive to criticism, and not very tolerant of correction.

In 1827, at the age of forty-four, we find him in Spain. He loved Spain. Some of his best work was done there.

The precincts of the Alhambra never failed to inspire him with lovely images and inexhaustible topics of romance.

There he wrote his best stories, told his best anecdotes, and exhumed from those archives, in which Mr. FROUDE has since laboured so admirably, the materials for some of his most careful historical work.

In 1829 he was Secretary of Legation at St. James's; in 1831 Chargé d'Affaires.

In 1832 he returned to America, and seems to have got into a most wretched and dejected state, whether from ill health, disappointed affection, or sense of diplomatic inefficiency, we cannot tell.

All through his biography we find these desponding moods from time to time recorded, but often without comment or explanation.

On his return to America he was received with open arms. His literary fame had preceded him—but IRVING was a bad popular idol.

He hated public speaking ; refused to address the Lyceum ; and even in private gatherings of friends, this most genial of men viewed the company with a jaundiced eye the instant he became aware that a speech was expected from him. "That Dickens's dinner—that Dickens's dinner!" he often said, with a memorial shudder : he had broken down miserably on that occasion, and never forgot the humiliation.

In New York "his time was cut up," he says, "like chopped hay."

He seemed to pine for rest and quiet.

In 1834 he made a tour in the prairies, and ended by settling down (he was now fifty-three) at Sunnyside, his country farm, with his sister and her children.

Here comes out that passionate love of open-air country life which seems to be planted in the breast of every true American, and lies deeper down even than his love of commerce and "Stores."

We see it in the regrets of the great President WASHING-TON, who gave up so much when he left his farm, his horses, his crops, his fishing and hunting, for the troubled life of a revolutionary camp.

We find it in the pages of EMERSON, who is never tired of the "refulgent summer, in which it is luxury to draw the breath of life in the midst of the fields spotted with gold and crimson fire."

In LOWELL, who can hear—

"The slender clarion of the unseen midge ; "

and mark how—

C

> " The rich milk-tingeing buttercup
> Its tiny polished urn holds up,
> Filled with ripe summer to the edge. "

In WARD BEECHER, whose rarest similes are derived from the corn-field, the flower-garden, seed-time and harvest.

In LONGFELLOW, who so loves "the murmuring pines and the hemlocks," the "little squirrel," "the wild roses of the promontories," and " the incessant sobbing of the sea."

In BRYANT, who comes to us—

> " Shaking a shower of blossoms from the shrubs,
> And bearing on their fragrance.   So he brings
> Music of birds, and rustling of young boughs,
> And sound of swaying branches, and the voice
> Of distant waterfalls. "

IRVING indulges even in bucolics. He writes to his niece : "You must contrive to come up soon, if only to see my new pigs."

But from such delights he finds himself, in 1841, "roughly, rudely summoned by a heartless destiny."

He leaves his roost at Sunnyside for the post of Ambassador to Spain.   "It is hard—very," he writes, whimsically, "yet I must try to bear it ! "

With touching recollections of rustic folds and bleatings of sheep about his native hills, he observes that "God tempers the wind to the shorn lamb ; " and his one idea seems to be to go to Madrid and come back with money, "and put up as many weathercocks as he pleased," all over the farm.

His stay at Madrid is marked more by delightful letters than recondite policy.

We hear all about the little Spanish queen, only thirteen, and her younger sister, and the ambassador seems chiefly occupied at court in "conjuring up nothings to say to little girls. This," he adds, "is the whipped syllabub of diplomacy."

Then there was the wicked old queen-mother, CHRISTINA, who had such charming manners and was always up to mischief; and the little nieces were never tired of hearing about what the princesses and great court ladies wore, and how they looked, and what they said and did.

In short, the ambassador's attention, if we may trust his own letters to the little girls at home, must have been largely devoted to bonnets and ribbons, Spanish lace, and such-like things, in which advanced and learned audiences at the Royal Institution can hardly be expected to take much interest.

But the poor little dears at the farm, far away by the Hudson river, knew no better, and doted on the good uncle's gorgeous talk about Spanish finery and court trappings.

And what an uncle that was! How great and important! how kind, and simple, and loving, and tender!

I think all good men love children—as THACKERAY says all good women love match-making. With Uncle WASHINGTON it was always "his dear, darling, restless little Kate," or "that pebble-hearted little woman," and he was ever "longing to return to his little flock at Sunnyside," and "put up those weathercocks."

In Spain he passed his time between literature, diplomacy, and the gout; but after suffering many things at the hands of many physicians, in 1845 his health seems to have taken a turn, and he chronicles this welcome improvement with a characteristic exclamation of gratitude—

"God bless those surgeons and dentists! May their good deeds be returned upon them a thousandfold! May they have the felicity in the next world to have successful operations performed upon them to all eternity!"

But the home hunger now became irresistible.   From the
midst of the gay court at Madrid the ambassador writes—

"I long to be once more at dear little Sunnyside, while I have yet
strength and good spirits, to enjoy the simple pleasures of the country,
and to rally a happy family group once more about me."

In 1846, at the age of sixty-three, he leaves the Spanish
capital, and returns, full of honour, fame, and not without
fortune, to his native land.

His public life was virtually at an end, and a life of more
variety and less exciting incident can scarcely be imagined.
He was familiar with Paris and London; Scotland, Germany, Switzerland, and Spain he had travelled through in
turn.

Everywhere he had been received by the *élite coteries* of
fashion, of literature, politics, arts, and sciences. He was on
terms of more than diplomatic intimacy with crowned heads,
but he delighted most in many humbler associations.

He knew the theatre and the counting-house, the rural life
of England, the delights of Alpine adventure, the prairies
and happy hunting-fields of wild Arkansas.

He had mingled in civic fêtes and popular celebrations.
He was regretted in London, Paris, and Madrid, and beloved
in New York and Boston; yet, amidst all these varied
scenes and tempting situations, he remained unspoiled—
simply the kind brother, the idolized uncle, the quiet literary
gentleman longing for his roost at Sunnyside by the Tappan
Sea.

WASHINGTON IRVING certainly retired on a competency.
As ambassador of course he received a liberal salary, and
his expenses in Spain could not have been very great.

His English copyrights alone won him 12,217 dollars, and
his other literary earnings about 24,500 dollars, making in

all a literary life-work which cannot be estimated at less than 36,717 dollars.

His declining years were spent in revising, re-editing, and collecting his scattered essays into miscellanies, and in writing the " Life of WASHINGTON," in four volumes.

He gives us a peep of himself now and then, trudging about his farm, or—

" Dozing over a book, girls all silently sewing around me."

But he was afflicted, like all men of literary ability, with the peculiar penalties of such greatness. His correspondence was oppressive :

· " All sorts of letters from all sorts of people."   " They tore his mind from him in strips and ribbons."

And then there were no post-cards in those days, and people had not mastered the brief slap-dash style of reply, but were still long-winded, stately, and verbose.

But what to do with all these post pests, numerous as summer gnats at sunset, it was hard to say.

Now it is a lady-writer, who has "some poems " she wants to publish ; another requests from IRVING just " one " original thought ; another inquires after "the exact place where RIP VAN WINKLE went to sleep in the Kaatskill Mountains ;" and—

" Each letter is a cobweb woven across your nose."   " The bores of this world," he exclaimed, "are countless ! "

Surprising to say, that, like the DUKE OF WELLINGTON, he answered most of these boring missiles.

" A man as he grows old," he remarked to his nieces, " must take care not to grow musty or fusty or rusty—an old bachelor especially."

In 1853 the clock of time has struck seventy. It finds him still hale and hearty ; but the shadows are lengthening.

He surprises himself going through that strange inevitable routine that awaits every one of us if we live so long.

He sits with the old ladies with whom he had danced fifty years before ; watches the little belles of six or thirteen ;. and marks out his own quiet resting-place in the neighbouring churchyard.

His passion for horse exercise often got him into trouble,. and he had eight or nine very narrow escapes.

Like many active old men, he continued from habit, perhaps pride, to take enterprising rides across country, when the response of nerve and muscle had become too slow to make such feats quite safe.

At seventy-two, he was thrown from a favourite but over-spirited animal called " Gentleman Dick," alighting upon his head.

"My horse became very rhetorical ; he tried," so he writes to a friend, " to shut me up like a telescope."

He gets over this fall ; but the inevitable cough, that familiar precursor of natural collapse, now appears.

He has a great longing to finish his "Life of WASHINGTON," but seems conscious of failing powers.　In writing the last volume, he says, " I could see how it ought to be done, but could not do it."　Yet the book is vigorous enough and able to the close.　So his life wore peacefully away.

Presently comes the sleeplessness and low spirits, against which he struggles manfully.

But IRVING had met the enemy who was to throw him at last.

Yet throughout his illness a certain Diedrich Knickerbocker humour never forsook him.

" Getting ready to go," he said ; " shutting up doors and windows."

And to his niece one morning, who asked him how he felt—

"I am apt to be rather fatigued; my dear, with my night's rest "—

which reminds me of the old lady who thanked God, and was sorry to say "she enjoyed very bad health !"

One night, late in the autumn of 1859, his favourite niece Sarah came in, as she was wont, to smooth his pillow before leaving him with that worst of companions, a restless solitude.

"When will this end ? " he said, half out loud.

She turned suddenly to look at him.

But the "end" had already come.

He fell forward, with his hand pressed upon his heart, and in another moment WASHINGTON IRVING, the accomplished writer, the genial humorist, the illustrious citizen, had ceased to breathe.

I am not here dealing with IRVING the historian, biographer, or mere tale-teller, but mainly with IRVING the humorist. As such, I notice that he had the singular fortune to write before all the good jokes had been made.

He is the first of the American humorists, as he is almost the first of the American writers ; yet, belonging to the New World, there is a quaint Old World flavour about him.

He is refreshingly deliberate ; never in a hurry.

Like BYRON'S "gentleman," he "never perspires."

He takes his time, and tells you his story in his own way.

The most delightful of gossips, the most ingratiating of "Roundabouts."

There is a good deal of the "Guardian," "Tatler," "Spectator," and old coffee-house wit and wisdom about him. But though sometimes gossipy, he is never flimsy, like so many of our modern magazine writers of "padding."

He knows how to be solid, to choose his words, to look all round his thoughts, to have thoughts that will bear looking at.

His wit is never forced ; he is seldom on the broad grin.

In him, indeed, are germs of an American humour since run to seed in buffoonery; but he is never outrageous —always within delicate bounds.

His fun never goes mad, but is in excellent subordination to his narrative or discourse.

His wit plays about his subject like summer lightning. His laugh, or more often his grave smile, rises naturally, and is never affected ; he is never strained or flashing, but often full of a deep and pathetic purpose ; and his jokes, when they come, seem woven into the very texture of his style, instead of sticking up outside like a cocked hat !

We have seldom the rollicking fun of DICKENS, but often a touch of his tenderness.

It is the satire of SWIFT, without his sour coarseness.

The grace of STERNE, without his sham sentiment.

The delicate flavour of CHARLES LAMB, without, however, the sly but severe bite of LAMB'S satire.

The chief fountains of IRVING'S humour are his "Sketch-book," containing the famous story of "Rip van Winkle," "The Legend of Sleepy Hollow," and the incomparable narrative of "The Headless Horseman."

"Bracebridge Hall," with its genial "Bachelor Confessions ;" its "Culprit," warm with the life-blood of humanity and gentle pity ; and its unique story of the "Stout Gentleman," which was so admired by CHARLES DICKENS.

The Knickerbocker's comic " History of New York," of which I shall give you a few specimens ; and " Wolfert's Roost," with its sketches in Paris, and general literary sweepings up. We have no right to complain.

Towards the end of his life, a man will often publish odds and ends that *he* does not think much of himself, but which he knows the public will be glad to buy, because *it* thinks much of him.

If I ask what is the secret of IRVING'S power, I find it to lie in a certain quiet absorption and concentration.

He identifies himself absolutely with whatever he is about ; a man is always attractive and interesting if he will do that.) As a consequence, we get a photographic minuteness of detail, the graphic points always being instinctively selected for the high lights.

He describes what he sees in his mind's eye, but his vision is clear and his observation accurate, down to the hue of a ribbon or the curl of a periwig.

Along with this object-painting goes the quaintest choice of adjectives and substantives, appropriate to the variety and vigour of the image evoked.

He is full of pithy wit and terse sayings, meditative occasionally, but not retrospective or metaphysical ; invariably graphic, scenic, objective, rousing an image which we usually recognize, and are generally glad to meet with.

But there is nothing so dull as a description of why and how a thing is written, especially when you can have the thing itself.

I will, therefore, pick out a few bright specks, and present you with some characteristic flashes of his wit, and then proceed to the graver task of suffusing you with at least two atmospheres of his humour, which I may as well describe at once as the *Moral* and the *Ordinary.*

First for a few specimens of the bright specks of colour, the flashes of wit, the pithy hits.

WASHINGTON IRVING'S portrait gallery would be a good subject for DU MAURIER'S pencil.

Who has not had the misfortune to sit next—

"The diner-out of first-rate currency when in town, who has been invited to one place because he has been seen at another"?

Who does not number amongst his acquaintances the widow of no particular age—

"Free, rich, disconsolate"?

Pages of description could do no more for her. The felicity of the adjectives recalls POPE'S graphic use of substantives in describing a lady's boudoir-table—

"Puffs, powders, patches, Bibles, *billet-doux;*"

or here we have the once inevitable but now less frequently to be met with social nuisance—the young lady in or out of her teens, who was always invited after dinner,

"To skylark it up and down the piano."

The coachman—a type unhappily not yet extinct amongst us—who only drives out—

"When he thinks proper; not when you want the carriage, but only when, in his opinion, it is good for the cattle."

And who has not met, coming down Bond Street or Regent Street just at the most crowded part of the afternoon, the middle-aged spinster, carefully leading by a string which gets round everybody's legs—

"The fat spaniel, Zephir, who is fed out of all shape and comfort"?

When ere I take my afternoon walks in St. James's, or lounge down "the sweet shady side of Pall Mall, with a couple of dukes," as THACKERAY used to say, I can see, looking out of their bow windows, those club bores, which IRVING hit off long before the historian of snobs.

" The men from India, who come home burnt out with curry, touched with the liver complaint ; who are so tediously agreeable in each other's society, with their ancient talk about the policy of Lord Ellenborough, the condition of the Punjaub, and the battle of Mulligatawny."

And who, as he wanders in the London season from drawing-room to drawing-room, is not familiar with the—

" Look of the man who has the oppressive burden of providing other people's amusement on his mind " ?

But these are squibs, and IRVING can burn his wit as long as a Roman-candle when he pleases.

What a bright jet of sustained and scintillating wit is that description of the old country gentleman, in the old parish church !—

" Who thought that religion belonged to the Government party, and was a very excellent thing, and ought to be kept up. When he joined so boldly in the service, it seemed more by way of example to the lower orders, to show them that, though so great and wealthy, he was not above being religious. 'As I have seen,' added Irving, 'a turtle-fed alderman swallow publicly a basin of charity soup, smacking his lips at every mouthful, and pronouncing it "excellent food for the poor."'"

I pass from these flashes, and enter into what I may call some of the humorous atmospheres of his mind.

When we suffuse ourselves with these, when we are caught in the meshes of his mood, we seem to come into closer and more continuous contact with his genius.

We are sensible of his power to influence, to impregnate, to inspire us with sympathy, indignation, disgust ; his piercing disclosure of shams ; his pity for the oppressed and fallen ; his sense of justice, his eagerness to strike a blow for the Right, whilst utterly holding up to ridicule and contempt the Wrong ! This you will lay to heart, and be often reminded of Porson's dictum, that "wit is the best sense in the world."

KNICKERBOCKER'S "History of New York" illustrates all the above qualities on a large scale.

The story of the early American settlers naturally possesses an undying interest for all Americans.

DIEDRICH KNICKERBOCKER'S comic history is a feat of playful and sustained satire, as far as I know without a parallel.

It is a fine example of the moral employment of humour.

Whilst you are kept in a constant simmer of laughter, you are reminded in every page that the writer has something to teach, if not to preach—something which you are to lay to heart; and when you close the book, through all the "good things" and "witty episodes" rings out the deep undertone of mournful rebuke and solemn warning.

I might cull, by the way, a good deal of quaint and severe wisdom, which by no means applies to New York alone or to KNICKERBOCKER'S time merely.

His account of diplomacy is edifying enough.

"It is," he says, "a cunning endeavour to obtain by peaceful manœuvres and the chicanery of cabinets those advantages which a nation would otherwise have wrested by force of arms; in the same manner as a conscientious highwayman reforms and becomes a quiet and praiseworthy citizen, contenting himself with cheating his neighbours out of that property which he would formerly have seized with open violence."

The following description of a treaty is good—good enough, alas! for even these enlightened times :—

"Treaties at best are but complied with so long as interest requires their fulfilment. Consequently, they are virtually binding on the weaker party only; or, in plain truth, they are not binding at all."

But perhaps the wittiest and saddest pages of KNICKERBOCKER are those in which he relates how the Dutch settlers turned the Red Indian out of his happy hunting-fields, stole his pastures, and appropriated his goods and chattels, with a full statement of the wise and moral reasons for so doing.

Under cover of pretended defence, we have here a complete *exposé* of the unscrupulous manner in which the European invader stole the land, and the unblushing arguments which he used in his defence. The question was—

"What right had the first discoverers of America to land and take possession of a country without first gaining the consent of the inhabitants, or yielding them an adequate compensation for their territory? . . . The first source of right was DISCOVERY. For as all mankind have an equal right to anything which has never before been appropriated, so any nation that discovers an uninhabited country, and takes possession thereof, is considered as enjoying full property and absolute, unquestionable empire therein."

The next thing, of course, is to prove that America was totally uninhabited by man.

"This would at first appear to be a point of some difficulty, for it is well known that this quarter of the world abounded with certain animals that walked erect on two feet, had something of the human countenance, uttered certain unintelligible sounds very much like language—in short, had a marvellous resemblance to human beings. But the zealous and enlightened fathers, who accompanied the discoverers for the purpose of promoting the Kingdom of Heaven, . . . soon cleared up this point, greatly to the satisfaction of his holiness the pope, and of all Christian voyagers and discoverers. They plainly proved—and as no Indian writer arose on the other side, the fact was considered as fully admitted —that the two-legged race of animals before mentioned were mere cannibals, detestable monsters, and many of them giants; which last description of vagrants, since the time of Gog, Magog, and Goliath, have been considered as outlaws, and have received no quarter in history, chivalry, or song. Being thus satisfactorily proved to be of 'a most abject and brutified nature, totally beneath the human character,' it was clear to the pious invaders, that the aborigines, so far from being able to own property, had no right even to personal freedom; and, being mere wild beasts of the forest, should, like them, be either subdued or exterminated."

The next right was that acquired by CULTIVATION.

"It is true that the savages might plead that they drew all the benefits from the land which their simple wants required." But that only proved "how undeserving of the blessings around them; they were so much the more savage for not having more wants. It is the number and magnitude of his desires that distinguishes the man from the beast."

Further, it was in the name of CIVILIZATION itself that the land was taken from the Indians, for—

"Not only were these poor creatures deficient in the comforts of life, but, what was still worse, most piteously and unfortunately blind to the miseries of their situation. But no sooner did the benevolent inhabitants of Europe behold their sad condition, than they immediately went to work to ameliorate and improve it. They introduced among them rum, gin, brandy, and the other comforts of life; they likewise made known to them a thousand remedies by which the most inveterate diseases are alleviated and healed; and, that they might comprehend the benefits and enjoy the comforts of these medicines, they previously introduced among them the diseases which they were calculated to cure."

But, of course, more important still was the introduction of CHRISTIANITY.

"It is true, the natives neither stole nor defrauded. They were sober, frugal, continent, and faithful to their word; but though they acted right habitually, it was all in vain unless they acted so from precept. The new-comers, therefore, used every method to induce them to embrace and practise the true religion—except, indeed, that of setting them the example."

Lastly, there came "the right by EXTERMINATION, or by GUNPOWDER." That was the most conclusive of all, and it is unnecessary to dwell further upon it.

"Thus," he concludes, "were the European worthies who first discovered America clearly entitled to the soil. And not only entitled to the soil, but likewise to the eternal thanks of those infidel savages for having come so far, endured so many perils by sea and land, and taking such unwearied pains for no other purpose but to improve their forlorn, uncivilized, and heathenish condition; for having made them acquainted with the comforts of life ; for having introduced among them the light of religion ; and, finally, for having hurried them out of the world to enjoy its reward ! "

It would be difficult to give a more grave and pathetic summary of all the injustice and tyranny of the white man over the red; and I may add of the selfish iniquity of political annexation generally, when the annexers have no real rights to claim, and leave the annexed none to grant.

I pass from the *moral* to the *ordinary* atmosphere.

The characteristic humour of " The Stout Gentleman," and the class to which that essay belongs, rises entirely out of the commonest of commonplaces.

A country Inn, a Traveller, and a Sensation.

But there is a depth of intense concentration thrown into the narrative which, slight as it may be, gives the episode rank with some of the best imaginative writing in our language.

The mind colours all things.

We carry about with us what we are to see and hear.

When I read this famous " Stage Coach Romance " of "The Stout Gentleman," I am actually at that wayside hostel in that gloomy month of November.

" That wet Sunday in the country inn " is throughout a rare creation. The view from the window—"the place littered with wet straw, which had been kicked about by travellers and stable-boys ; " a corner of the yard, with its "stagnant pool of water surrounding an island of muck ; " its · "miserable, crestfallen cock, drenched out of all life and spirit, his drooping tail matted as it were into a single feather, along which the water trickled from his back," and· so on for another admirable two pages, full of minute photography.

A flash of relief comes with the arrival of the stage-coach, which deposits its freight, and whisks off again in the wet.

Our traveller now saunters listlessly to the almanack hanging up in the inn parlour, and, looking at the month, reads a direful prediction, stretching from the top of the page to the bottom, through the whole month: " Expect—much—rain —about—this—time ! "

I cannot hope to paraphrase what follows :—

"I was dreadfully hipped. The hours seemed as if they could never creep by. The very ticking of the clock became irksome. At length the stillness of the house was interrupted by the ringing of a bell. Shortly after, I heard the voice of a waiter at the bar, 'The Stout Gentleman in No. 13 wants his breakfast. Tea and bread and butter, with ham and eggs ; the eggs not to be too much done.'

" In such a situation as mine every incident is of importance. Here is a subject of speculation presented to my mind, and ample exercise for my imagination. I am prone to paint pictures to myself, and on this occasion I had some materials to work upon. Had the guest upstairs been mentioned as Mr. Smith, or Mr. Brown, or Mr. Jackson, or Mr. Johnson, or merely as '*gentleman in No.* 13,' it would have been a perfect blank to me—I should have thought nothing of it ; but 'The Stout Gentleman ! '—the very name had something in it of the picturesque. It at once gave the size ; it embodied the personage to my mind's eye, and my fancy did not rest.

" He was stout, or, as some term it, lusty ; in all probability, therefore, he was advanced in life, some people expanding as they grow old. By his breakfasting rather late, and in his own room, he must be a man accustomed to live at his ease, and above the necessity of early rising ; no doubt a round, rosy, lusty old gentleman.

"'There was another violent ringing. The Stout Gentleman was impatient for his breakfast. He was evidently a man of importance ; 'well to do in the world ;' accustomed to be promptly waited upon ; of a keen appetite, and a little cross when hungry. 'Perhaps,' thought I, 'he may be some London alderman ; or who knows but he may be a member of Parliament ? '

" The breakfast was sent up, and there was a short interval of silence ; he was doubtless making the tea. Presently there was a violent ringing ; and before it could be answered another ringing, still more violent. 'Bless me ! what a choleric old gentleman !' The waiter came down in a huff. The butter was rancid, the eggs were overdone, the ham was too salt. The Stout Gentleman was evidently nice in his eating ; one of those who eat and growl, and keep the waiter on the trot, and live in a state militant with the household."

The smart hostess, after scolding the servants, sends up another breakfast, which appears to be more graciously received. Then the bell rings again. The Stout Gentleman wants the *Times,* or the *Chronicle.* Was he a Radical or a Conservative ? Who could he be ? "Rain—rain—rain ! I now read all the advertisements of coaches and hotels that were stuck about the mantelpiece. . . . I wandered out, not knowing what to do, and ascended again to my room."

"I had not been there long, when there was a squall in a neighbouring bedroom. A door opened and slammed violently ; a chambermaid, that I had remarked for having a ruddy, good-humoured face, went downstairs in a violent flurry. The Stout Gentleman had been rude to her.

"This sent a whole host of my deductions to the deuce in a moment. This unknown personage could not be an old gentleman ; for old gentlemen are not apt to be obstreperous to chamber-maids. He could not be a young gentleman ; for young gentlemen are not so apt to inspire such indignation. He must be a middle-aged man, and confoundedly ugly into the bargain, or the girl would not have taken the matter in such terrible high dudgeon. I confess I was sorely puzzled.

"In a few minutes I heard the voice of my landlady. I caught a glance of her as she came tramping upstairs, her face glowing, her cap flaring, her tongue wagging the whole way. 'She'd have no such doings in her house, she'd warrant ! If gentlemen did spend money freely, it was no rule. She'd have no servant-maids of hers treated in that way, when they were about their work ; that's what she wouldn't !'

"As I hate squabbles, particularly with women, and above all with pretty women, I slunk back into my room, and partly closed the door ; but my curiosity was too excited not to listen. The landlady marched intrepidly to the enemy's citadel, and entered it with a storm ; the door closed after her. I heard her voice in high windy clamour for a moment or two. Then it gradually subsided, like a gust of wind in a garret ; then there was a laugh ; then I heard nothing more.

"After a little while, my landlady came out with an odd smile on her face, adjusting her cap, which was a little on one side. As she went

D

downstairs, I heard the landlord ask her what was the matter; she said, 'Nothing at all, only the girl's a fool.' I was more than ever perplexed what to make of this unaccountable personage, who could put a good-natured chamber-maid in a passion, and send away a termagant landlady in smiles. He could not be so old, nor so cross, nor so ugly either."

So the day wears on in such-like rambling and restless conjecture. "The continual meditation on the concerns of this invisible personage began to have its effect—I was getting a fit of the fidgets." The excitement is now steadily worked up, upon less than nothing at all, until it reaches the agony point, and the reader is finally released in fits of laughter.

"Dinner-time came. I hoped the Stout Gentleman would dine in the travellers' room, and that I might at length get a view of his person ; but no ! he had dinner served in his own room. What could be the meaning of this solitude and mystery? He could not be a radical ; there was something too aristocratical in thus keeping himself apart from the rest of the world, and condemning himself to his own company throughout a rainy day. And then, too, he lived too well for a discontented politician. He seemed to expatiate on a variety of dishes, and to sit over his wine like a jolly friend of good living. Indeed, my doubts on this head were soon at an end ; for he could not have finished his first bottle before I could hear him faintly humming a tune, and on listening, I found it to be ' God save the King.' 'Twas plain, then, he was no radical, but a faithful subject ; one that grew loyal over his bottle, and was ready to stand by king and constitution, when he could stand by nothing else. But who could he be ? My conjectures began to run wild. Was he some person of distinction travelling *incog.* ? ' Heaven knows !' said I, at my wits' end ; ' it may be one of the royal family, for aught I know, for they are all stout gentlemen !'

" The evening gradually wore away. The travellers read the papers two or three times over. Some drew round the fire, and told long stories about their horses, about their adventures, their overturns and breaking-downs. They discussed the credits of different merchants and different inns ; and the two wags told several choice anecdotes of pretty chamber-maids and kind landladies. All this passed as they were quietly taking what they called ' night-caps,' strong glasses of brandy-and-water and sugar, or some other mixture of the kind ; after which they one after the other rang for ' Boots ' and the chamber-maid, and walked off to bed in old shoes cut down into marvellously uncomfortable slippers.

" There was only one man left ; a short-legged, long-bodied, plethoric fellow, with a very large sandy head. He sat by himself, with a glass of port wine negus, sipping and stirring, meditating and sipping, until nothing was left but the spoon. He gradually fell asleep bolt upright in his chair, with the empty glass standing before him ; and the candle seemed to fall asleep too, for the wick grew long and black, and cabbaged at the end, and dimmed the little light that remained in the chamber. The gloom that now prevailed was contagious. Around hung the shapeless and almost spectral box-coats of departed travellers, long since buried in sleep. I only heard the ticking of the clock, with the deep-drawn breathings of the sleepy toper, and the drippings of the rain, drop, drop, drop, from the eaves of the house. The church bells chimed midnight. All at once the Stout Gentleman began to walk overhead, pacing slowly backwards and forwards. There was something extremely awful in all this, especially to one in my state of nerves—these ghastly greatcoats, these guttural breathings, and the creaking footsteps of this mysterious being. His steps grew fainter and fainter, at length died away.

"I could bear it no longer. I was wound up to the desperation of a hero of romance. ' Be he who or what he may,' said I to myself, ' I'll have a sight of him ! ' I seized a chamber candle, and hurried up to No. 13. The door stood ajar. I hesitated—I entered. The room was deserted. There stood a large broad-bottomed elbow-chair at a table, on which was an empty tumbler and a *Times* newspaper, and the room smelt powerfully of Stilton cheese.

" *The mysterious stranger had evidently but just retired.* I turned off, sorely disappointed, to my room, which had been changed to the front of the house. As I went along the corridor, I saw a pair of topboots, with dirty waxed tops, standing at the door of a bedchamber. They doubtless belonged to the unknown ; but it would not do to disturb so redoubtable a personage in his den ; he might discharge a pistol, or something worse, at my head. *I went to bed*, therefore, and lay awake half the night in a terribly nervous state ; and even when I did fall to sleep, I was still haunted in my sleep by the idea of the Stout Gentleman and his waxed topboots.

" I slept rather late the next morning, and was awakened by some stir and bustle in the house, which I could not at all at first comprehend ; until, getting more awake, I found there was a mail-coach starting from the door. Suddenly there was a cry from below, ' The gentleman has forgotten his umbrella ! look for the gentleman's umbrella in No. 13 ! ' I heard an immediate scampering of a chamber-maid along the passage, and a shrill reply, as she ran, 'Here it is! here's the gentleman's umbrella!'

"The mysterious stranger was then on the point of setting off. This was the only chance I should ever have of knowing him. I sprang out of bed, and scrambled to the window, snatched aside the curtains, and just caught a glimpse of the rear of the person getting in at the coach-door. The skirts of a brown coat parted behind, and gave me a full view of the broad disk of a pair of drab breeches. The door closed— 'All right!' was the word; the coach whirled off; and that was all I ever saw of the Stout Gentleman!"

II.

OLIVER WENDELL HOLMES.

II.

OLIVER WENDELL HOLMES.

SOME acts are interesting because of the actors, and some actors are interesting because of their acts :

An observation, as ARTEMUS WARD would say, requiring some thought, but one which will amply repay attention.

As far as I can gather, the public exploits of Dr. OLIVER WENDELL HOLMES do not call for special remark; they derive their interest almost entirely from the man.

OLIVER WENDELL HOLMES was born at Massachusetts in 1809, he is therefore seventy-three years old (1882). He graduated at Harvard in 1829.

He tried the law, like WASHINGTON IRVING, but soon exchanged the uncongenial pursuit of briefs for the more delightful occupation of writing prescriptions; and after studying medicine in Paris (1833), returned to Boston (1836), and became Professor of Anatomy at Dartmouth, United States of America, in 1838, and at Harvard in 1847.

After a medical practice of little more than fifteen years, he retired in 1849; and in the most insensible and spontaneous manner, by scattered writings, witty and wise speeches, and pleasant, often funny, poems and epigrams, has won for himself a foremost place in that very small band of American *littérateurs* by whom the nineteenth century will be remembered.

In every page of his writings I trace the influence of his medical and scientific training.

Yet there is nothing of the narrow specialist about him.

He is an almost passionate physiologist, but no materialist.

He bows reverently to the inexorable logic of cause and effect, yet acknowledges depths of Being undreamt of in medical philosophy.

He loves fact, yet often salutes with awe the superior angel of imagination. Nor does he forget, amidst the iron tyrannies of experimental philosophy and the tremendous Empire of the Senses, the insoluble mystery and immense Supremacy of the Soul.

In winter Dr. HOLMES lives at Boston, the Brain of the United States. In summer at a private estate of his own, beautifully situated on the Housatonic River, Pittsfield, Massachusetts.

In America it seems to be the custom, at anniversaries and "inaugurations," to get eminent literary persons to write and recite poems.

Such a thing is almost unknown in this country. Fancy Mr. TENNYSON or Mr. BROWNING reciting a poem on the opening of the Channel Tunnel or the International Exhibition !

On such occasions, we invite Mr. GLADSTONE or Mr. BRIGHT to make a speech, and our *vers d'occasion* are relegated to small literary societies—the Sheldonian Theatre or the Cambridge Senate House on degree days.

But metrical essays are, or were, all the rage across the water.

BRYANT, EMERSON, LONGFELLOW, HOLMES, and LOWELL have in turns distinguished themselves in this way.

The *North American Review*, and later, the *Atlantic Monthly*, sparkled with many poems and essays from Dr. HOLMES's pen.

He wrote also prize essays on fever, homœopathy, and such-like cheerful topics, ever scintillating with that shrewd prying, sympathetic curiosity and suggestiveness which gives such a personal, almost conversational, flavour to all his writings.

How shall I finish this meagre biographical paragraph?

I had better say that there is little more to be said, until we are favoured with an autobiography by Dr. HOLMES himself.

I will add that, meanwhile, Allibone's Dictionary of Biography contains two columns of praise, in which OLIVER WENDELL HOLMES is compared to SPENSER, POPE, DRYDEN, HOOD, DICKENS, and almost every one else whom it is in the least worth while being compared to—a biographical method which, if a little uncritical and "mixed" in tone, is a very good way of saying that Dr. OLIVER WENDELL HOLMES, whatever Posterity (for whose opinion he would probably care very little) might think, was in the estimation of his contemporaries clearly A 1 as a man and a writer.

I shall never be able to regard HOLMES as, first and foremost, a Poet, although a vein of poetry and admirable sentiment runs through all his prose.

I shall say he is first Essayist, and Poet afterwards; and this because he is never "rapt," never quite caught up into Heavens inaccessible to ordinary fancy and baffling to common intelligence.

He is, indeed, full of intuition, but far too reflective ever to be quite inspired.

The "Metrical Essay" and "Astræa" resound with high strains, and his longer poems contain bright bursts of patriotism and noble religious utterances, as well as those sudden transitions to satire and almost low comedy, which remind one of poor ROBSON's fitful moods.

I would that he had written more lyrics.

I believe that such exquisite verses as the " Violet" and the " Water-lily" the world will not willingly let die.

He is so far a didactic *and* lyric poet.

In America HOLMES has acquired a great reputation as a writer of *vers de société.*

His longer efforts in this direction remind me of a class of lampoons and satires more fashionable in the days of BYRON and TOM MOORE than in ours; and it is curious to note that, whilst America may be considered generally a good fifty years ahead of Europe in many of her social and commercial phases, in her literature she still relishes, both for prose and poetry, the essay style of WASHINGTON IRVING, and the epigramamtic satire of POPE, which received its last English rehabilitation at the hands of HAZLITT.

This description of two persons meeting in the street is altogether in POPE's manner—

> " Each looks quite radiant, seems extremely struck,
> Their meeting so was such a piece of luck !
> So then they talk, in dust or mud or snow,
> Both bored to death, and both afraid to go. "

Or this timely slap in the face for America—

> " Thou, O my country, hast thy foolish ways !
> Too apt to purr at every stranger's praise ;
> But if the stranger touch thy modes or laws,
> Off goes the velvet, and out come the claws. "

These are from his longer satires. They are little read in England, where so many of their allusions can hardly be relished or even understood. The popularity in America of his comic skits must also be largely due to local and personal causes.

They belong to a class of which we have had more than enough.

We always like a good fellow to get up at a supper-party or a dull wedding-breakfast, and make a clever speech, and perhaps even recite a facetious poem.

We can sometimes, in intimate circles of men, especially when the edge of taste is not very sharp, tolerate a song; but few of such ebullitions of the hour are worth transplanting, and many, like Mr. SPURGEON's jokes, lose their point when repeated outside.

In this *genre* HOLMES seems to me below HOOD in fertility, whilst the "Spectre Pig" and the "Ballad of the Oyster-man" are hardly equal to many of BON GAULTIER's Ballads or HORACE SMITH's "Rejected Addresses," although I admit that the "Organ Grinder"—whilst inferior to CALVERLEY's inimitable poem—is nevertheless very excellent fooling.

But Dr. HOLMES's great charm is, after all, his own personality.

He really "sees himself in all he sees," and he makes us feel that we cannot see too much of him.

He has selected his literary vehicle with the surest tact.

His favourite method is *unique* in its handling and application. It is announced in one phrase, " THE AUTOCRAT OF THE BREAKFAST TABLE."

The American boarding-house is in many respects different from anything that we have in this country, chiefly on account of the very varied classes who are willing to meet and associate for a time on equal terms, and the very superior people who occasionally find a *modus vivendi* there congenial to themselves.

The "Professor," the "Autocrat," and the "Poet at the Breakfast Table" are summed up in three volumes, now universally popular.

Of these the "Autocrat" is the first and most widely read; the "Professor" is, to our mind, the best; and the "Poet" is the mere after-glow of a method which the writer himself seems to feel is at last played out. He has, in fact, by the time he figures as the "Poet," said very nearly all he has to say.

The "Autocrat" is his own Boswell. He talks and talks, and the rest chime in occasionally. As the breakfasts succeed each other, the doings of the subordinate characters develop into something like a plot, which culminates sadly in the "Professor" with the death of the real hero, and gladly in the "Autocrat" with the marriage of that oracular but genial person himself.

The characters, though slight—mere pegs for wit and wisdom, as some might say—are all put in with such vivid touches, that they get quite alive after the first two or three mornings.

We have the vulgar gentleman with the dressy—too dressy—waistcoat, blue-black moustache, showy cravat, and large diamond pin. He is called appropriately the Koh-i-noor.

There is the anxious landlady, nervous about finance, solvent lodgers, and the "staying" power of the dishes when they show a tendency to give out before completing the round.

There is the pale and interesting young schoolmistress, whose cheeks are nevertheless capable of colouring up under appropriate circumstances, such as I may have to allude to presently.

There is a strange little deformed gentleman, full of oddity and intellect, whose talk is always incisive, trenchant, caustic, and interesting—full of keen sensibility, and with a certain covered vein of tenderness which relieves the

enduring bitterness and sense of general failure and disappointment riveted upon him by his unhappy personal
deformity.

And then, in the "Professor at the Breakfast Table," we
have that most charming of all Dr. HOLMES's creations, the
lovely Iris—a bright sunny blonde, with shining hair, and
a radiant joyousness, — most winning in her moods of
touching and spontaneous sensibility ; a pure, deep, passionate soul, with great width and tenderness, and a certain
divine simplicity which makes her the innocent bright angel
of the book.

I know nothing in CHARLOTTE BRONTË finer than the
delicate *rapprochement* which takes place between the lovely
Iris and the little deformed gentleman ; and the whole
account of his rapid decline and death is equal to any
piece of romance-writing—I had almost said biography—
that I have ever read.

But although the episodes in the "Professor" are more
highly wrought than in the "Autocrat" or the "Poet," the
charm of all three books is the same.

All are so many masks—living masks, but under the
writer's perfect control ; not like THACKERAY's characters,
often rebellious, saying and doing all kinds of things which
surprise the author, and compel him to follow instead of to
lead.

These masks are pushed aside at any moment, thrown
down and taken up, interrupted, silenced, or encouraged, as
occasion or the humour of the moment may demand.

But even when the mask is on, the kind face of OLIVER
WENDELL HOLMES is wont to peep through—sad sometimes
with pathos and pity, as when the great procession of unloved
women, the lonely, the forsaken, the forlorn, the suffering,
passes before him ; filled sometimes with large and wise

toleration for the erring and sinful ones; bowing reverently before the painful riddle of this earth, yet sensitive to every vibration of the human heart; keenly open to life at all points, "with its great glad aboriginal instincts," its bursts of passion, its healthy joyousness, its sad despairing undertones, its noble sacrifice; and, lastly, I notice throughout the most shrewd and delicate insight into character, born of wide sympathies and unrivalled powers of observation.

I shall now put together what I may call a short mind-biography of OLIVER WENDELL HOLMES.

I always like to realize the kind of man I have to deal with.

It helps me to read his books, and to read them aright.

I like to feel the teacher at my elbow, especially this teacher; to look round and find him near, with his grave kind face, his beautiful smile—his eye flashing indignation at wrong, brightening at generosity or heroism, and not incapable of shedding a manly tear over human folly, weakness, or misfortune.

If you want to take the general bearings of a man's soul, you have only got to ask and answer, if you can, a few leading questions, such as—

First, what are his Ideals; what does he admire or detest most,—love most to be or to do?

Second, what kind of Religion has he got?

Third, what views does he take of his own profession and its general Aims?

Fourth, how does he think and speak about Women?

First, Ideals.

"A man's opinions, look you," says Holmes, "are generally of much more value than his arguments."

Which reminds me of a letter I once received from a clever editor, along with a manuscript "returned with thanks," as follows :—

"DEAR SIR,

"I offer you no apology or explanation in returning your manuscript, for my experience has taught me that, whereas an editor is usually right in his decision, he is invariably wrong when he attempts to give his reasons.

"Yours, etc."

A man's opinions are wont to form his Ideal. His reasons for his opinions are often made up later, and they may be good, bad, or indifferent.

"Once fix a man's ideals, and for the most part the rest is easy. A wants to die worth half a million. Good! B, female, wants to catch him and outlive him. All right! Minor details at our leisure."

No number of high-flown considerations will mend that situation or save that character.

HOLMES is generous in his estimates, but generosity does not exclude severity.

The loving heart can pour forth its scorn upon meanness, and he who well knows how to pardon Frailty can stamp with a pitiless heel upon Dishonour.

There are some actions which mar and stain a man to the core; there are some sins which have no forgiveness, neither in this world nor in the world to come.

Let a man once deliberately commit himself to such and such a meanness, as we sometimes see done under the sun; let him barter honour, purity, the happiness of others— not for passion, not in weakness, not even for ambition, that last infirmity of noble minds, but for *pelf*, for *filthy lucre*, for Iago's "get money in thy purse!"—and such a character goes down for ever in the opinion of all good men.

Others may flatter him, crowds may attend his receptions and eat his dinners, but there is one whose verdict is not to be bought. He stands apart, and we will stand with him, and hear the tale.

What? eh? You say he married for money, and it

was on such wise, thus : threw over a woman, gave up, sold, bribed, lied—nay, perjured himself—and *did it for money ?* All right ! keep your apologies, spare your " extenuating circumstances." " Minor details at our leisure."

Ah ! let the cynic and mere selfish utilitarian say what he will, there is something in the passionate love of goodness that wins the ear of the ages and masters the heart of man from generation to generation.

It is the infallible test by which we involuntarily weigh the greatest spirits. MOSES, SOCRATES, PAUL, and above these the DIVINE MAN, are all safely enthroned ; and on other pinnacles, which scarcely reach up to their pedestals, come, lower down, ALEXANDER, CÆSAR, NAPOLEON, HOMER, GOETHE, and even SHAKESPEARE.

No one is a more enthusiastic admirer of genius than OLIVER WENDELL HOLMES; but his ideal is moral, not intellectual, and he proclaims aloud, sometimes perhaps without being aware of it himself, the glories of a kingdom not of this world.

Thus, after a glowing eulogy upon Genius, he exclaims, with the contagious fervour of irresistible conviction—

" And yet when a strong brain is weighed with a true heart, it seems to me like balancing a bubble against a wedge of pure gold."

Our Age is sometimes called Materialistic and Utilitarian —in the sensual and selfish senses of these words.

But is it nothing to live at a Time when, in spite of all, the popular idols are still based upon the Supremacy of Moral Excellence ?

It is enough ; it is everything.

In this America is fortunate, distinguished, and incalculably influential.

Do not EMERSON, LONGFELLOW, HAWTHORNE, LOWELL, and HOLMES all ring true to the Supremacy of the Moral and Spiritual nature of man ?

Watchwords often of mere narrowness—the very catspaws of Sectarian bigotry.

Yet do I find nothing priggish, puritanical, or repellant in the writings of these typical Americans.

HOLMES is singularly companionable, and, as the French say, *intime.* We feel that he is so delightful, that we long to trust him "all in all," and we may do so safely.

There is nothing about him to be left out, hardly a word' or an utterance that I desire to modify, nor a counsel I can afford to disregard.

He is not like BYRON, who dazzles us, or SWIFT, who domineers over us, or STERNE, who trifles with us, nor is he a mere wag, like some of the later American humorists; but he is one to rest in, to travel with. We love to have him close to us—our welcome guide, philosopher, and friend.

Second, Religion

If any one asked Dr. HOLMES, as it is said a lady once asked Dr. JOHNSON, "Pray, what is your religion?" he might possibly answer in the words of the English sage—

"Madam, I am of the religion of all sensible men."

"And pray what is that?" said the lady.

"That, madam," he replied, "is a thing which all sensible men keep to themselves."

And yet HOLMES is far from keeping it all to himself. It creeps out in little wise aphorisms, such as—

"Faith always implies the disbelief of a lesser fact in favour of a greater."

Sometimes it pierces through the thin veil of narrative, as when the divinity student approaches the sick-bed of the little deformed gentleman, and finds in him a master rather than a disciple.

" 'Shall I pray *with* you?' he said after a pause. A little before, he

E ,

would have said, 'Shall I pray *for* you?' The Christian religion, as taught by its Founder, is full of sentiment; so we must not blame the divinity student if he was overcome by those yearnings of human sympathy, which predominate so much more in the sermons of the Master than in the writings of his successors—which have made the parable of the prodigal son the consolation of mankind, as it has been the stumbling-block of all exclusive doctrines. ' Pray,' said the little gentleman."

And the prayer that follows is so sweet and solemn, so deep and tender, and so purely religious, that it may hardly find a place in a lecture on an American humorist.

But HOLMES is a man who needs, above all, to be looked at all round. His very humour is deeply interwoven with serious elements, and this last interview of the divinity student with the little gentleman, in which the tables are so suddenly turned, and theology stands abashed before the religion of the heart, is in itself one of the deepest strokes of pathetic humour.

After this, we need not be surprised to find that, whilst ignoring the various theological *isms*, which do so much more to divide than to unite the hearts of the faithful, HOLMES has the liveliest sympathy with all earnest worshippers, and quite a love for religious assemblies in general.

" 'I am,' says the Professor—and we can scarcely mistake the voice that speaks—'a regular churchgoer. I should go, for various reasons, if I did not love it; but I am happy enough to find great pleasure in the midst of devout multitudes, whether I can accept all their creeds or not.' "

I suppose, if we must label our subject, he must be labelled "Broad Church," although I should be disposed to claim something a great deal more significant, definite—dogmatic, if you will—under that name than he would probably agree to.

" The Broad Church, I think, will never be based upon anything that requires the use of language. Freemasonry gives the idea of such a

Church. The cup of cold water does not require to be translated for a foreigner to understand it. The only Broad Church possible is that which has its creed in the heart, and not in the head."

I should be tempted to add to without impairing this definition, by saying, "Ay, but in the head too, and on such and such wise, for of the fulness of the heart the mouth speaketh, and the head will ever insist upon formulating and reformulating the thoughts and feelings that are ever struggling up into spoken and written language."

Hence the glory of poets, philosophers, and preachers.

Does not some one nearer home teach us very well thus ?—

> " Though truths in manhood darkly join,
> Deep-seated in our mystic frame,
> We yield all honour to the Name
> Of Him that made them current coin."

Third, his Profession.

I like to know how a man views his daily occupation.

Whether he grumbles at it, lounges through it, uses it mechanically to live by, or lives in it, and learns by it, and loves it.

It is easy to see, in almost every page of HOLMES's writing, that he loves the doctor's profession because he loves human nature, and this helps him to study it in manifold byeways, to explore its secrets, to sound its heights and depths, and to minister like a kind angel to its weakness, pain, and sorrow.

"'I have heard it said," he writes, "that the art of healing makes men hard-hearted, and indifferent to human suffering. I am willing to own that there is often a professional hardness in surgeons, just as there is in theologians, only much less in degree than in these last. A delicate nature will not commonly choose a pursuit which implies the habitual infliction of suffering, so readily as some gentler office ; . . . yet you may be sure that some men, even among those who have chosen the task of pruning their fellow-creatures, grow more and more thoughtful and truly compassionate in the midst of their cruel experience. They become less nervous, but more sympathetic; they have a truer sensibility for others' pain, the more they study pain and disease in the light of science. I have said this without claiming any special growth in humanity for myself, though I do hope I grow tenderer in my feelings as I grow older."

When I read this, I felt that I should like to have Dr. OLIVER WENDELL HOLMES to attend me. I think I should often feel a little poorly.

Fourth, Women.

I remember W. F. ROBERTSON, of Brighton, saying somewhere that there are two rocks upon which a soul may be wrecked—GOD and the opposite sex.

Indeed, as to the first, we can know little about a man until we know his general tone of thought about religion—as apart from the state of theological opinion at home or abroad; nor can we know a man at all well until we can give some account of his general tone of feeling about women—quite apart from the marriage laws or social conventions at home or abroad.

I will at once put aside the male icicle, the man who is comparatively insensible to female attractions.

In either sex you will find individuals of every degree of sensibility, and you will as often find the female icicle given up to proud, perhaps useful, spinsterhood or wretched matrimony, as you will find the born bachelor, to whom female society in any form appears to be either an accident or an aimless superfluity.

But there are men with such a quick vein of sensibility that in women's society they seem to be half women themselves, without, strange to say, losing one wit of manliness.

This combination may be rare, but it is by no means *unique.*

In an unapproachable degree it existed in the Blessed Author of the Christian religion.

This type, often quite as fascinating to men as to women, is as far as the poles removed from maudlin sentimentalism.

It invariably means such an intense and immediate recognition of the essential psychology of men and women, such an intuitive knowledge, admiration, and love for the noblest, and such a tender pity for the weak and erring, that for the time the human heart is like a mirror, and sees reflected within itself the image that confronts, absorbs, and is absorbed by it.

The secret of DE BALZAC'S enormous popularity was simply this, the whole womanhood of France—not a very pure, but a very passionate, vigorous, and, to a great extent, a suffering and oppressed race of women—felt that at last they were described by a man who understood them, and who estimated them not above, but certainly not below, their real worth.

DE BALZAC did this by a prodigious feat of sympathetic imagination. He had never lived through what he described, any more than MASSILLON or LACORDAIRE had lived through the sins they so eloquently analyzed and denounced.

DE BALZAC saw bits of womanhood alive, and was well acquainted with the morbid anatomy of dead love.

His genius enabled him to live in an ideal world—a world that became so real to him that he demanded no other.

Into this world he summoned the living, breathing types of women who lived and moved and had their being in that real world, with which he had so little to do.

You may say he lived with the shadows of women, not with women. Be it so; he nevertheless became their confessor, their consoler, and their immortal portrait-painter.

The sympathy which in DE BALZAC was ideal, is most simple, earnest, and real in OLIVER WENDELL HOLMES, and his taste is far purer.

His belief in women is boundless; his love is wise; his admiration sincere, innocent, open.

He often sketches them at full length, and still more often seizes a half length, three-quarters, or profile.

He surprises them in tears; and grows light at heart and jubilant when he sees their fresh girl-faces wreathed in smiles.

He is always respectful, always generous, sometimes a little sly, but never undignified.

The Professor is asked—

"Did I believe in love at first sight? 'Sir,' he exclaims, and there is an almost Johnsonian ring about the gravely frivolous reply, 'all men love all women—that is the *primâ facie* aspect of the matter. They are so bound in duty and inclined by nature.' Then, in a vein of sustained humour, he goes on to say that if there are any lawful exceptions to the above rule, the man is bound to stand forth at the bar of our common humanity, and show cause why he does not love any given woman. He may plead that he has not seen her; that she is a blacka-moor, or ill-favoured, or of tender age; or, lastly, that he is in love already, and then he will stand excused."

But he does not always jest on the subject, and his deep reverence for women is constantly allowing itself to be divined.

"There are at least three saints among the women to one among the men."

And his very reverence begets in him an extreme and more than oriental jealousy, but it is a jealousy of their souls, more than of their bodies.

He is never so near being hard and exacting as when demanding the highest of a creature, so compounded of snow and flame that she seems at any moment ready to rise to the loftiest peaks or plunge into their corresponding abysses.

Often, beneath a vein of tender exaggeration, we feel something of the Othello grip of a man fiercely in earnest with a being whom he feels to be at once sublime and frail.

> "I would have a woman as true as death. At the first real lie, which works from the heart outward, she should be tenderly chloroformed into a better world, where she can have an angel for a governess, and feed on strange fruits, which shall make her all over again, even to her bones and marrow."

Like WASHINGTON IRVING, THACKERAY, and all people who connected women's rights with the bloomer costume, a glass of water, and a green cotton umbrella, OLIVER WENDELL HOLMES is a little hard on strong-minded ladies and over-education.

He has a very keen feeling of the atmosphere, the mind-tendency, and the sort of activities most appropriate for women.

No doubt, we have lived to see much of the early exaggeration of the woman's rights movement drop away, and we claim to have retained its solid benefits in the shape of improved legislation and a healthier view of what is due to women as members of the body politic.

In fact, we are just now (1882) in the midst of that new phase in the woman's rights movement, which turns on the higher education of women—and I fear this, too, is in danger of going a little wild.

I do not care, any more than does HOLMES, for the preponderance of the head over the heart in women.

The type of schoolgirl-boy, with its long stride, its bag, and its books in a strap, indifferent to female grace and haughty about marriage—though, it may be, not quite recalcitrant—does not, as the French say, "smile to me."

I should be thrifty of sarcasm at any movement which women thought likely to improve their social or political condition.

I should certainly encourage girls to read and take an

interest in general literature or science ; but, as far as I see, OLIVER WENDELL HOLMES is substantially sound on the great woman's question, right and left, and in his own charming and tender way he utters the words of soberness and truth when he says—

"The brain women never interest us like the heart women : white roses please less than red."

Yet are HOLMES'S women no fools, like THACKERAY'S. His charming Iris is full of imagination and intelligence, and his schoolmistress is above the average in mind as well as in sensibility and personal grace.

But whilst idolizing, as he evidently does, what GOETHE called the "evig weibliche"—"the eternal feminine"—he knows how to be fair and generous to the exceptional women with masculine, or at least supra-feminine minds.

"We owe a genuine tribute of respect to those filtered intellects, who have left their womanhood on the strainer.   They are so clear that it is a pleasure at times to look at the world of thought through them ; *but the rose and purple tints of richer natures they cannot give us.*"

If he has ever jested or spoken unadvisedly with his lips about any of them, if he has been a little arbitrary or exacting, if he has insisted upon seeking the excellences of all women in every woman, and turned away disappointed to find that each woman lacked something, he stands forgiven ; he makes his peace with the whole sex at the close of that pathetic passage in which the dear ministering angel of suffering humanity is painted, spending herself very willingly, and being spent, in those gentle charities which solace so many pains, and rob even death of some of his terrors—

"God bless all good women !   To their soft hands and pitying hearts we must all come at last !"

As I look back upon this rapid mind-sketch of OLIVER

WENDELL HOLMES, the nature of his ideals, the practical character of his religion, his large-hearted sympathy with men, women, and children, I can only say, " Heaven send us on this side of the Atlantic a teacher so wise and generous, so witty, so tender, and so true ! "

You may open any of the three volumes upon which HOLMES's fame really rests, the " Autocrat," the " Professor," or the " Poet," and find on every page aphorisms and epigrams which deserve to be framed, put down in your private note-book, or carried in your heart.

I will transcribe a few specimens before proceeding, in a more systematic way, to note some flashes of his wit, atmospheres of his humour, and a fugitive, very fugitive glimpse of his novel-writings.

MEMORY.—" Memory is a net. One finds it full of fish when he takes it from the brook, but a dozen miles of water have run through it without sticking."

CONTROVERSY.—" Controversy equalizes fools and wise men in the same way—and the fools know it."

UNPOPULAR OPINION.—" A man whose opinions are not attacked is beneath contempt ; "

and

" Every real thought on every real subject knocks the wind out of somebody or other."

TENDENCY.—" I find the great thing in this world is not so much where we stand as in what direction we are moving."

SECRETS.—" We never tell our secrets to people who jump for them."

FAME.—" Fame usually comes to those who are thinking about something else ; rarely to those who say to themselves, ' Go to, now ! let us be a celebrated individual ! ' "

PRAISE.—"You may set it down as a truth which admits of few exceptions, that those who ask your opinion really want your praise."

SINCERITY.—"Why can't somebody give us a list of things which everybody thinks and nobody says, and another list of things that everybody says and nobody thinks?"

THE RED INDIAN.—"A few instincts on legs, flourishing a toma-   \
hawk."

His keen insight flashes out in many bright, brief, and admirably smart reflections ; things we have often thought, never said.

Hear him on comedy and tragedy—

"Wonder why authors and actors are ashamed of being funny? Why there are obvious reasons, and deep philosophical ones too. The clown knows very well that the women are not in love with him, but with Hamlet—the fellow yonder in the black coat and the plumed hat. Passion never laughs ! The wit knows that his place is at the tail of the procession."

And here the balance of the situation is wisely kept, the true relation of comedy to life defined, with a practical tact which the comic man would at all times do well to ponder.

" If the sense of the ridiculous is one side of an impressible nature, it is very well; but if that is all there is in a man, he had better have been an ape, and stood at the head of his profession at once."

On one occasion, it is said, Mr. SPURGEON, being accused of a certain levity in the pulpit, was not eager to deny the soft impeachment, whereupon his censor, waxing indignant, exclaimed—

"I wonder, sir, how you, a minister of the gospel, can venture to utter so many witticisms in the house of God."

"Ah !" said the great preacher, with a pathetic little sigh, " you wouldn't if you knew how many I keep to myself."

Still, there was some force in the objector.

It is very difficult for a really funny man to get credit for being anything else. The risible faculties are easiest stirred ; we are more prone to laugh than to cry, and more prone to do either than to think.

A wit who means to be taken seriously must beware of being too witty too often or too soon.

" Keep your wit in the background," says HOLMES, " until you have made a reputation by your more solid qualities : you will do nothing great with Macbeth's dagger, if you first come on flourishing Paul Pry's umbrella."

I like to repeat PORSON's definition of wit—" the best sense in the world." How much wisdom lies in a witty proverb, how much condensed meaning in a terse epigram !.

HOLMES is never happier than when wrapping up his dose of thought in such an elegant gilt bolus as this—

MONEY.—" Put not your trust in money, but put your money in trust."

There is a whole sermon in the first clause, " Put not your trust in money," and it may be preached on the text " the love of money is the root of all evil ; " and the whole philosophy of thrift is in the last, "put your money in trust." The secret of a sound investment is not the least important lesson to teach an age gone mad with " Rings " and suffering from bubble companies on the brain.

People travel a good deal now—Americans for cheapness, Germans for instruction, French for pleasure, and English it is impossible to say for what ! But one experience is common to them all ; it is this—

" Travellers change their guineas, not their characters."

Travel shows people to themselves and to each other. Their character may not change, but " going about " often brings out their latent peculiarities.

Once across the Channel, perhaps even before we get as

far, we try conclusions and draw distinctions with our friend, not always without a difference.

We knew he was lazy before, but we had no notion that he would not get up to see a sunrise or to catch the train.

We knew he liked his dinner, but for the Alhambra or the Pyramids we thought dinner might wait.

Well, at the end of the first week, he denounces you as radically unsound on the commissariat question; and in a fortnight, he takes to his bed, and will do nothing but smoke. " Men change their guineas, not their characters ! "

Alas ! the application can be made still more personal. How many of us rush abroad to drown anxiety or sorrow, to get rid of ourselves, we require only " change of air ! " Miserable cheat ! a mere shallow cry got up, like the Rhine castles and the live chamois goats, for the Cooke tourists. You change your guineas sure enough, and take your ticket ; you are well over the water, you will enjoy the change.

Ha ! who is that on the pier, who comes to meet you as you land ?

Why, it is the same dismal, woebegone figure that you left a hundred miles behind you.

" What ! " cries Emerson, " travellest thou so fast in the earth, old mole ? "   Even so !   *You* are the old mole, none other ; or, as ALFRED DE MUSSET poetically says—

> " Partout où j'ai touché la terre,
> Sur ma route est venu, s'asseoir
> Un malheureux vêtu de noir,
> Qui me ressemblait comme un frère. "

In the more prosaic words of OLIVER WENDELL HOLMES, " Men change their guineas, not their characters ! "

A horsey country like ours will appreciate the following uncompromising, or perhaps rather compromising statement :—

HORSES.—" He who is carried by horses must deal with rogues."

My own experience is that there are three things about which even good men have no conscience at all.

The first is horses.

The second is violins.

The third is umbrellas.

But, as I am in this cynical mood, let me finish and have done, for it is not a vein congenial to the spirit of our Autocrat, or to the warm summer life and the genial humanity which habitually suffuses his soul.

I will, therefore, allow him to utter but one last cynicism, at once mercenary and sentimental, on MATRIMONY :

> "Quoth Tom, 'Though fair her features be,
>   It is her figure pleases me.'
> 'What may her *figure* be ?' I cried.
> '*One hundred thousand*,' he replied."

No one understands atmospheres better than HOLMES.

He will plant his seed in a certain soil, and it will develop after its kind. Do what you will, you can only see with his eyes for the time. You go round and round his plant—it develops and enlarges, but, like the flower out of a soil which has been tampered with chemically, it comes up all mauve or magenta, instead of white or red.

THE DEVELOPMENT OF THE HAT.

Certain objects act upon HOLMES like the red flag on a bull. Amongst these is the " HAT."

It always excites him. I should like to know what kind of hat OLIVER WENDELL HOLMES is in the habit of wearing. Who is his hatter ?

I would venture to say he inclines more to the straw and wideawake than to the chimney-pot.

It is nevertheless the chimney-pot hat which he contemplates with an almost vicious complacency of satire.

It evidently possesses for him a certain dangerous fascin-
ation ; he cannot let it alone.

A new hat, a shabby hat, a squashed hat, an old hat, each
in turn attracts him, as the feather in the ladies' turban used
to attract poor SOTHERN when he came in as Garrick
feigning drunkenness.

Now he is in mock heroics—

> " Have a good hat.   The secret of your looks
> Lives with the beaver in Canadian brooks.
> Virtue may flourish in an old cravat,
> But man and nature scorn the shocking hat ! "

Or it is the damaged hat that is developed in three
sententious propositions thus—

First, " A hat which has been popped by being sat down upon is
never itself again afterwards."

Second, " It is a favourite illusion of sanguine natures to believe the
contrary."

Third, " Shabby gentility has nothing so characteristic as its hat.
There is always an unnatural calmness about its nap, and an unwhole-
some gloss suggestive of a wet brush."

He is equally happy on

THE DEVELOPMENT OF THE BUN.

" In order to know whether a human being is young or old, offer it
food of different kinds at short intervals."

The crucial experiment is this—

" Offer a bulky and boggy bun to the suspected individual just ten
minutes before dinner. If this is eagerly accepted and devoured, the
fact of youth is established ; if the subject of the question starts back
and expresses surprise and incredulity, as if you could not possibly be
in earnest, the fact of maturity is no less clear."

I will give but one more example of a perfectly whimsical
atmosphere, in which Holmes has had the wit to place another
common human thing—a thing as common and human and
familiar to us all as the hat or the bun.

It is THE COUGH.

"Coughs are ungrateful things. You find one out in the cold; you take it up, nurse it, make everything of it, dress it up warm, give it all sorts of balsams, and other food it likes, and carry it round in your bosom as if it were a miniature lap-dog. And by-and-by, its little bark grows sharp and savage, and—confound the thing!—you find it is a wolf's whelp that you have got there and he is gnawing in the breast where he has been nestling so long.

I can merely glance at HOLMES as a novelist. If I do not select for comment "The Guardian Angel" or "Elsie Venner," it is not because I do not recognize their merits.

As novels they are not strong, but they are full of fragmentary studies of character and situations of genial and sometimes of weird fancy. If not unique, they are in many ways remarkable.

The conception of "Elsie Venner" belongs almost entirely to the sphere of medical psychology.

Strange animal tendencies are the commonplaces of insanity, and we may have noticed in human beings odd facial likenesses to animals which have gone more than skin-deep.

This borderland of mystery is just the one in which HOLMES's genius would be likely to revel, and a girl with the tendencies of a snake is quite the sort of person our philosopher would wish to describe and analyze.

And he has done it. Still, the genius of HOLMES will remain to the end desultory, fragmentary, capricious, and incapable of any sustained effort which would prevent him from flying off at some opportune tangent.

From which it results that his desultory books are full of sustained interest, whilst his novels are, in spite of their power and originality, dull.

That is why I take my specimens of his novel-writing from two books which are not novels.

The sketch of Iris from the " Professor," and the sketch of the Schoolmistress from the "Autocrat."

A writer who wants to describe a woman, and who understands his business, does not go through the catalogue of her charms. He knows better. He means *you* to do that for him, and to do it better than he could. He draws for each character upon the whole of your past experience; he puts in a touch here and a touch there, which suggest to you a vast deal more than even he dreams of.

He tells you, for instance, of a blonde—a particular kind of blonde; not a cold blonde, with hair like tow, but a blonde with the summer through her blood, and the warm —not the cold—white complexion, and the shining hair with that gloss as of yellow floss silk that holds the light.

You know exactly the sort of girl. All the beautiful blondes you have ever seen rise in your mind as you read, or rather a mental combination of them begins to glow and radiate out upon you from the cunning novelist's pages, and the thing is done.

And so, too, he will treat you with a brunette, and all the beautiful brunettes you have ever seen will give her their charms.

Or he will paint you the gown fitting close about the white throat of one of those delicate, pale but not sickly creatures—too sedentary, too thoughtful, scarcely alive to their own depths; unawakened, but quite ready to be awakened; sensible, quiet, and sensitive, and a little too slight, and there you have the young governess in the " Autocrat."

But first let us have Iris.

Nothing can be more subtle than the way in which she is indirectly sketched, from her cradle to the fulness of her glowing and sunny-hearted girlhood. Can anything exceed the fineness of touch which, in a few lines, describes her poor mother's death and her own birth?

"The poor lady (thy mother), seated with her companion at the chess board of matrimony, had but just pushed forward her one little white pawn (Iris) upon an empty square, when the black knight that cares nothing for castles or kings or queens, swooped down upon her and swept her from the larger board of life."

Iris appears about seventeen or eighteen at the boarding-house, and almost insensibly gravitates to the one inmate most remotely opposite to herself.

She takes her seat at breakfast always by the side of the little deformed gentleman, whose brilliant conversation she loves to hear, and who grows more brilliant and original as she listens sympathetically.

Iris read and thought too. She was an artist. She had a precious diary and a still more precious sketch-book. She had her secret thoughts, and yearnings, and aspirations, and ideals, and sadnesses, young as she was.

"A child? yes, if you choose to call her so—but such a child! Do you know how art brings all ages together? There is no age to the angels and ideal human forms among which the artist lives, and he shares their youth until his hand trembles and his eye grows dim. But why this lover of the beautiful should be so drawn to one whom Nature has wronged so deeply seems hard to explain. Pity!—I suppose they say that leads to love."

Undoubtedly Iris was full of character. She was not a *negative*, but a *positive* blonde, with the golden tint running through her.

"Come, probably enough, from those deep-bosomed German women that TACITUS portrayed in such strong colours."

Though positive, she was intensely receptive. Something of the little deformed gentleman's own peculiar energy and mental vigour seemed at times to be reflected in her. She had an odd temperament, too; was given to sleep-walking.

One of her pretty trances is prettily told, and is a little

F

weighted with an abnormal mesmeric suggestion. It was on this wise :—

The little gentleman, it appears, was very strong in his shoulders and arms; his hand could hold you like a vice. The Professor meets Iris in her night-walking, asleep. Awaking from her trance, " she took my hand. 'I feel,' she said, 'as if all my strength were in this arm.'" She tightened her grasp in the Professor's hand.

"Good heavens! she will crack my bones! All the nervous power of her body must have flashed through those muscles! Iris turned pale, and the tears came to her eyes. She saw she had given me pain. Then she trembled, and might have fallen but for me. The poor little soul had been in one of those trances which belongs to the spiritual pathology of higher natures, mostly those of women."

The pathetic relation between the poor little, embittered, deformed gentleman and the lovely, sympathetic Iris has now to be worked up. A few touches here and there suffice.

"One thing is sure—the interest she takes in her little neighbour is getting to be more engrossing than ever. Something is the matter with him, and she knows it, and, I think, worries herself about it."

Soon after, the Professor writes—

"I must tell Iris that her poor friend is in a precarious state. She seems nearer to him than anybody. I did tell her. Whatever emotion it produced, she kept a still face. . . . 'He shall have some of my life,' she said. A fancy, I suppose, of a kind of magnetic power she could give out. I cannot help thinking she wills her strength away from herself. I have sometimes thought he gained the force she lost—a whim very probably."

As the crisis approaches, we are, of course, put off in various ways, according to the Professor's peculiar and desultory method of treatment.

The deepening of Iris's character by contact with suffering is emphasized by the introduction of one of HOLMES's most delicate lyrics, "Under the Violets," said to have been found in the young girl's album.

"UNDER THE VIOLETS.

"Her hands are cold, her face is white;
   No more her pulses come and go;
Her eyes are shut from life and light.
   Fold the white vesture, snow on snow,
   And lay her where the violets blow.

"But not beneath a graven stone,
   To plead for tears with alien eyes:
A slender cross of wood alone
   Shall say that here a maiden lies
   In peace beneath the peaceful skies.

"And grey old trees of hugest limb
   Shall wheel their circling shadows round,
To make the scorching sunlight dim
   That drinks the greenness from the ground,
   And drop their dead leaves on her mound.

"When o'er their boughs the squirrels run,
   And thro' their leaves the robins call;
And, ripening in the autumn sun,
   The acorns and the chestnuts fall,
   Doubt not that she will heed them all.

"For her the morning choir shall sing
   Its matins from the branches high:
And every minstrel voice of spring
   That trills beneath the April sky,
   Shall greet her with its earliest cry.'

"When, turning round their dial-track,
   Eastward the lengthening shadows pass,
Here little mourners, clad in black—
   The crickets, sliding thro' the grass,
   Shall pipe for her an evening mass.

"At last the rootlets of the trees
   Shall find the prison where she lies,
And bear the buried dust they seize
   In leaves and blossoms to the skies.
   So may the soul that warmed it rise!

"If any, born of kindlier blood,
    Should ask, 'What maiden lies below?'
Say only this: 'A tender bud,
    That tried to blossom in the snow,
    Lies withered where the violets blow.'"

We are soon ushered into the little gentleman's sick-room—that strange, haunted apartmènt, which no boarder, except, perhaps—and only perhaps—the young girl, was ever allowed to enter.

One night the Professor, who had now become the invalid's medical man, on issuing forth from the sick-chamber, meets Iris in one of her trances.

This scene will bear no second description: it is a masterpiece of refinement, and the novelist is certainly here at his very best. He never does better, except, perhaps, in the pathetic last chapter of the little gentleman's life, to which I must now hasten on.

"'I know it all,' said Iris, his self-appointed nurse. 'He is going to die, and I must go and sit by him. Nobody will care for him as I shall, and I have nobody else to care for.'"

Soon after this, the divinity student pays the little gentleman a well-intentioned and kindly visit; but an allusion to his sins calls forth a last brilliant tirade from the little man, full of eloquence and pathos.

"'I have learnt to accept meekly what has been allotted to me, but I cannot honestly say that I think my sin has been greater than my suffering. I bear the ignorance and the evil-doing of whole generations in my single person. I never drew a breath of air, nor took a step, that was not a punishment for another's fault. I may have had many wrong thoughts, but I cannot have done many wrong deeds, for my cage has been a narrow one, and I have paced it alone. I have looked through the bars, and seen the great world of men busy and happy, but I had no part in their doings. I have known what it is to dream of great passions; but since my mother kissed me before she died, no woman's lips have pressed my cheek—nor ever will.' The young girl's eyes glitter with a sudden film, and almost without a thought, but with a warm human instinct that rushed up into her face with her heart's blood, she bent over and kissed him. It was the sacrament that washed out long years of bitterness, and I should hold it an unworthy thought to defend her. The little gentleman repaid her with the only tear any of us ever saw him shed.

"The divinity student rose from his place, and, turning away from the sick man, walked to the other side of the room, where he bowed his head and was still. All the questions he had meant to ask had faded from his memory. The tests he had prepared by which to judge of his fellow-creature's fitness for heaven seemed to have lost their virtue. He could trust the crippled child of sorrow to the Infinite Parent. The kiss of the fair-haired girl had been like a sign from heaven, that angels watched over him whom he was presuming but a moment before to summon before the tribunal of his private judgment."

I can afford to make the sketch of the schoolmistress much slighter. It will resolve itself into one or two sentimental touches and a love-scene—always the crucial test of a writer of fiction, and one in which HOLMES will not be found wanting.

The *dramatis personæ* are a gentleman of middle age—the Autocrat, in fact—with much of the vivacity of youth and more than the loquacity of age, which is a fair statement, as he talks almost uninterruptedly through two hundred pages of close print ; and the schoolmistress, that same pale young person, with the tight, neatly fitting dress close up to her neck, with a little bit of ribbon or flower to set off her delicate complexion,—not at all a sickly young woman, but perhaps suffering from a little over-attention to her class and suppression of young vigorous life, which sorely wanted a run in the fields or a ramble on the mountains and—and—well, it must be admitted, a manly bosom for the wise and gentle head to rest upon.

But HOLMES shall put her upon the canvas, with a few of his own effective strokes of the brush—

"The schoolmistress came down, with a rose in her hair, a fresh June rose. She has been walking early. She has brought back two others, one on each cheek."

The Autocrat—a decidedly staid, sober-minded, and philosophical gentleman—is much drawn to this young person.

He talks rather better when she is listening, and often looks for her approval, which he appears invariably to get.

In the free and easy life of an American boarding-house, nothing could be more natural than an occasional walk before or between school hours, and an occasional walk she and the Autocrat had together.

"'This is the shortest way,' she said, as they came to the corner.
"'Then we won't take it,' said I."

When they got home, he could not help noticing that her colour was a little heightened. It certainly became her.

"I felt sure," he adds, "it would be useful to her to take a stroll like this every morning."

The intelligent reader, after this, begins to look for the inevitable result, and is much relieved to read, after one or two such strolls—

"I'm afraid I have been a fool, for I have told as much of myself to this young person as if she were of that ripe and discreet age which invites confidence and expansive utterance."

However, he soon gets over this indiscretion, and decides that another morning walk would be good for him ; and, besides, the schoolmistress will be glad of a little fresh air before school.

He is, in fact, falling step by step an easy and willing victim, whilst most comically standing out for it that he never once made love to the young woman in any one of those walks. However, he is forced to admit that what he calls—

"The throbbing flushes of the poetical intermittent have been coming over me of late ; "

and the growing flame is fanned by the ingenuous ecstasy
of the schoolmistress at his glowing descriptions of distant
scenes, the glories of the Alps, and so forth.

" ' If I thought I should ever see the Alps,' said she.
" ' Perhaps you will some time or other.'
           " *Mental tableau.*

" [Chamouni—Mont Blanc in full view ; figures in the foreground ;
two of them standing apart, one of them a gentleman of—oh !—ah !—
yes !—the other a lady in a white cashmere shawl, leaning on his
shoulder, etc.]."

Of course, the drama can no more stand still at this point
than a rolling ball on an inclined plane, and we are quite
prepared for this style of thing—

" Once in a while one meets with a single soul," etc., etc. ;

Or—

" I saw that eye and lip and every shifting element were made for
love."

Naturally; but still this sophistical Autocrat has the
effrontery to reiterate—

" I never spoke one word of love to the schoolmistress in the course
of these pleasant walks."

Ah ! well, there are more ways than one of making love.
But the indefinite postponement, the endless digressions,
the Autocrat's moods, emotions, and their self-deceptions
are so agreeable that we are quite sorry to come, as come
we must, to the last walk !

" It was on the common that we were walking. The *mall*, or boule-
vard of our common, you know, has various branches leading from it in
different directions. One of them runs downward from opposite Joy
Street southward, across the whole length of the common, to Boylston
Street. We called it the long path, and were fond of it.

" I felt very weak indeed—though of a tolerable robust habit—as
we came opposite the head of this path on that morning. I think I

tried to speak twice without making myself distinctly audible. At last I got out the question—

"'Will you take the long path with me?'

"'Certainly,' said the schoolmistress; 'with much pleasure.'

"'Think,' I said, 'before you answer. If you take the long path with me now, I shall interpret it that we are to part no more.'

"The schoolmistress stepped back with a sudden movement, as if an arrow had struck her.

"One of the large granite rocks used as seats was hard by; it's one you may still see close to the giuko tree.

"'Pray, sit down,' I said.

"'No, no,' she answered softly; 'I will walk the *long path* with you!'

"The old gentleman who sits opposite met us walking arm-in-arm, about the middle of the long path, and said, very charmingly, 'Good morning, my dears.'"

III.

JAMES RUSSELL LOWELL.

III.

JAMES RUSSELL LOWELL.

MR. LOWELL says somewhere that the art of writing consists largely in knowing what to leave in the ink-pot.

We may add that the art of publishing consists largely in knowing what to leave in the waste-paper basket.

As an experienced editor, that is a discovery our author must have made long ago—but he has been too severe with himself.

How many volumes of LOWELL'S prose works, if not in the waste-basket, are almost as effectually buried in magazine and newspaper columns? How many ink-pots between 1838 and 1880 have been absorbed by the blotting-paper of oblivion?

A brief review of Mr. LOWELL'S working life will give the reader some notion of what the world has *not* got, and will serve to call attention to the condensed wealth contained in such unpretentious little volumes as "Among my Books," and "My Study Windows."

But the man must take precedence of his work.

The "LOWLES," from Yardley, Worcestershire, left Bristol

for America about 240 years ago. There was evidently
"stuff" in the family, as the town of "Lowell," a shire
town of Middlesex, Massachusetts, is named after them.

CHARLES LOWELL, a respected Unitarian minister at
Boston, was the father of the present poet, and determining
that his son JAMES RUSSELL should have a liberal education, he sent him to Harvard University, where he entered
at fifteen, became "Class poet," graduated at nineteen, and
on leaving college was recommended to study law.

Whether Mr. LOWELL's faculty for promoting litigation
was imperfect or insufficiently cultivated is of little consequence to posterity ; had he been a successful lawyer, he
might have become a professional politician—the world
would then have probably lost a poet and a statesman.

About a year seems to have satisfied him that human
nature, from a legal point of view, was unproductive—
perhaps dull.

At all events, in 1841 he published a collection of poems
called "A Year's Life." As they have never been re-
printed, and we have not seen the original volumes, they
may have been poetical digests of interesting cases. Some,
however, have been republished ; but we fail to find in the
exquisite plaint of "Threnodia," "Irene," "My Love," "To
Perdita, singing," or "The Moon," the least allusion to the
"Prisoner at the Bar," "Costs," or even a "Fee Simple."

The mature taste which cancels early work is not always
to be relied on.

Why Mr. TENNYSON should have only retained one
exquisite line in the whole of his prize poem "Timbuctoo"
—a poem full of mature and sustained beauty—is to us as
great a mystery as why Mr. RUSKIN seems anxious to bury
for ever in oblivion all his more important writings, which
the world, however, will not willingly let die.

However, "to fresh woods and pastures new," in company with Mr. ROBERT CARTER, did Mr. LOWELL betake himself in 1843, and the "Pioneer, a literary and critical magazine," supported by EDGAR POE, HAWTHORNE, PARSON, STOREY, and others, was pioneered through three monthly numbers, when the publisher failed, and the venture was wrecked.

Every one must buy his experience, and the interests of authors and publishers get a little mixed sometimes—especially those of authors—still, the great matter is to find one's "sea legs" on the voyage of literary life.

In 1844 the verses including "A Legend of Brittany," "Prometheus," "Rhœcus," and some sonnets, showed at least that the poet and philanthropist was beginning to stand firm upon that quarter-deck on which the great anti-slavery battle was to be fought and won.

In 1845 a prose volume of conversations appeared, on some old poets—CHAUCER, CHAPMAN, FORD, etc.—subsequently, I suppose, incorporated in "My Study Windows"—and various hints, paragraphs, and disquisitions on politics and slavery prepare the way for some patriotic bursts of feeling, the indignation and the eloquent wrath of "The Present Crisis" (1848), "Anti-Texas," and "On the Capture of certain Fugitive Slaves near Washington."

These were shortly followed, in that most momentous year '48, when the States were seething with revolution and Europe was in a blaze with LOUIS NAPOLEON's exploits, by "The Vision of Sir Launfal," and the famous "Biglow Papers." "A Fable for Critics" also appeared in the year '48.

In 1851 Mr. LOWELL visited England, France, and Switzerland, and lived for some time in Italy. Such essays as "Dante" show how deeply he imbibed the spirit of Italy's greatest poet, and how closely he studied the schools of Italian painting and the relics of the Roman or Greco-Roman sculpture.

Of the Greek sculpture there is little enough in Italy; only a few marble replicas of a few fine statues—the originals of all the finest Greek statues were in ivory or bronze.

He joins in the abuse of MICHAEL ANGELO at present fashionable, and the reader may be referred to the section on "Italy," printed in the "Fireside Travels," for a variety of *impressions de voyage*, probably unlike what was printed before them, but very similar to what has appeared since.

I miss the "flying grace" of HOWELL's "Venetian Life," but this Mr. LOWELL would call "cheapening" one thing by another; and then, indeed, the impress left by Italy upon his mind and studies is far more important than are any of the pleasant chatty notes made guide-book in hand.

One thing is certain, that Mr. LOWELL avoided travelling as other Americans are said to travel—seeing everything and looking at nothing—or, worse still, making notes, as they rush from place to place on the "Continong," of what they neither have seen nor looked at.

I remember myself meeting two such enterprising travellers when I was last in Rome. They were standing opposite the "Apollo Belvidere" in the Vatican. One held guide-book with pencil, and read; the other mastered as rapidly as he could the labels on each pedestal.

"Wal, what's the next?" says the American 'Arry with the guide-book.

"That," says his friend, stooping down to examine the label—"that's the 'Pollo Belvidere."

"Chalk 'im off," says his friend with the pencil, and both passed on without even raising their eyes to the Sun-god!

But to be at leisure, to master well, to think and write

maturely, is an old-world feature retained by Mr. LOWELL. It is one of his main charms; like good wine, it will keep—ay, and bear exportation to boot.

In December, 1852, he returned to America, and in 1854 and 1855 lectured on the British poets. The substance of these lectures probably reappeared in "Among my Books."

In January, 1855, on the resignation of Mr. LONG-FELLOW, Mr. LOWELL, by that time famous and influential as the poet of the "Biglows," accepted the chair of modern languages and *belles lettres* in the Harvard College.

With that passion for thoroughness which he had so humorously and forcibly expressed in the "Biglows," Mr. LOWELL revisited Europe to qualify himself especially in the French and German languages and literatures for his new post.

> " Folks thet worked thorough was the ones thet thriv,
>   But bad work follers ye ez long's ye live ;
> But can't git red on't—jest ez sure ez sin,
>   It's ollers askin' to be done agin."

To this period at Dresden, 1856, we doubtless owe those exhaustive studies, the fruits of which come out in the excellent essays on "LESSING" and "ROUSSEAU"—papers which impress the reader, without apparent effort or design, with the feeling that the writer knows so much more than he cares to say.

In 1857 to 1862 many essays, not since republished, appeared in the *Atlantic Monthly*, of which Mr. LOWELL became editor; and in 1863 to 1872 he edited, in conjunction with CHARLES E. NORTON, the *North American Review*—a kind of American "Revue des Deux Mondes" in literary importance.

In 1864 appeared the pleasant "Fireside Travels," containing his gossip about "Cambridge, U.S., 30 years ago;" "The Moosehead Journal," full of characteristic incidents and glimpses of out-of-the-way lonely scenery, and American travel in pleasant byways; experiences at sea, together with appearances of whales and jellyfish; a pensive paragraph on the sea-serpent, and a few words of sympathy for that rare monster's admirers; some notes on the Mediterranean, not unlike other people's notes on the Mediterranean, and " In Italy "—generally—very generally.

In 1867 we have the " Second Series of Biglow," and " Melibœus Hipponax;" in 1868, " Under the Willows, and other poems;" in 1869, " The Cathedral," an extensive poem redolent of foreign travel, but interspersed with those delightful meditations and serious reflections without which Mr. LOWELL's earnest nature is incapable of long exhaling itself in either prose or poetry.

In 1870 the pith of many essays and magazine articles is extracted and issued in his three chief prose volumes, " My Study Windows," and two volumes " Among my Books."

In 1872 Mr. LOWELL is again in Europe, and in 1874 Cambridge University—not U.S.A.—confers its LL.D. in the Senate-house upon one who certainly by this time, more by the quality than by the quantity of his books, had won for himself a foremost place in English literature, as well as a special throne in America, where he may well be called the Prize Poet of the Vernacular.

From the English point of view all this may seem an odd training for a politician. Indeed, our English House of Commons has always been a little shy of literary men (although it happens to have a good supply of them just now—1880). LORD MACAULAY was a fair parliamentary success as far as he went, but his extreme distaste for office perhaps betrayed a certain sense of unfitness to excel in practical politics. BULWER LYTTON was a showy *succès d'estime* as a debater.

JOHN STUART MILL, although unable to keep his seat, left his hall-mark on every question that he touched upon in the House.

LORD BEACONSFIELD was altogether an exceptional phenomenon, and his poet-statesmanlike appointments were equally phenomenal.

However, they manage all these things differently in America, and, indeed, they make politicians out of all sorts of stuff, for home use—but for foreign service a literary career seems to be no unnatural or unusual prelude.

Mr. HOWELLS was consul at Venice, so was G. P. R. JAMES ; Mr. BRET HARTE is consul at Glasgow. Mr. LOWELL, who had never made a political speech or sought his country's suffrage at home, or held any State appointment whatever, was offered the post of Ambassador to Russia in 1874, which he declined ; but so determined were the Americans to be represented by him abroad, that Madrid, which he accepted, was offered him in 1877, and London in 1880 ; nor could any better appointment have been made.

The style of Mr. LOWELL is emphatically his own, and yet no man reports so habitually — half sympathetically, half whimsically—the ring of other writers.

" Homer Wilbur " is especially redolent or resonant of the old Elizabethan Masters. We hear the grave VERULAM LORD BACON, or the judicious HOOKER, in—

" Our true country is that ideal realm which we represent to ourselves under the names of religion, duty, and the like. Our terrestrial organizations are but far-off approaches to so fair a model, and all those are verily traitors who resist not any attempt to divert them from their original intendment."

Sometimes we get an odd flavour of SWIFT, bright humour being substituted for malignant satire ; at others, the flowing and tender style of JEREMY TAYLOR comes back to us as we

G

read; and this pretty close to a quaint essay on Journalism is certainly the oddest mixture of EMERSON and STERNE :

"Through my newspaper, here, do not families take pains to send me, an entire stranger, news of a death among them? Are not here two who would have me know of their marriage? And, strangest of all, is not this singular person anxious to have me informed that he has received a fresh supply of Dimitry Bruisgins? But to none of us does the Present continue miraculous (even if for a moment discerned as such). We glance carelessly at the sunrise, and get used to Orion and the Pleiades. The wonder wears off, and to-morrow this sheet, in which a vision was let down to me from Heaven, shall be the wrappage to a bar of soap, or the platter for a beggar's broken victuals."

But here is a bit of the genuine, unadulterated LOWELL, in one of his rare bursts of terrible scorn and irony. It is indeed a tremendous indictment on the war material of an ' Unthrifty Mother State," this picture of a war recruit.

"An own child of the Almighty God! I remember him as he was brought to be christened—a ruddy, rugged babe ; and now there he wallows, reeking, seething—the dead corpse, not of a man, but of a soul—a putrefying lump, horrible for the life that is in it. Comes the wind of heaven, that good Samaritan, and parts the hair upon his forehead, nor is too nice to kiss those parched, cracked lips ; the morning opens upon him her eyes full of pitying sunshine, the sky yearns down to him, and there he lies fermenting. O sleep ! let me not profane thy holy name by calling that stertorous unconsciousness a slumber ! By-and-by comes along the State, God's vicar. Does she say, ' My poor, forlorn foster-child ! Behold here a force which I will make dig and plant and build for me ' ? Not so ; but, ' Here is a recruit ready-made to my hand, a piece of destroying energy lying unprofitably idle.' So she claps an ugly gray suit on him, puts a musket in his grasp, and sends him off, with Gubernatorial and other godspeeds, to do duty as a destroyer."

Mr. LOWELL is hard upon fine writers; and, indeed, his own style, although rising to an occasion, never approaches· the chronic elevation of the penny dreadful; he prefers "was hanged" to "was launched into eternity ;" he would have the poor taste to write "when the halter was put round his neck," rather than "when the fatal noose was adjusted about the neck of the unfortunate victim of his own unbridled passions;" he will not even call a "great fire" a "disastrous conflagration," or speak of "a frightened horse" as an "infuriated animal." Instead of rising at a public dinner with " I shall, with your permission, beg leave to offer some brief observations," Mr. LOWELL might have the poor taste to begin, " I shall say a few words."

But he never talks the current nonsense about good Saxon English, and he boldly maintains that our language "has gained immensely by the infusion (of Latinisms), in richness of synonym, and in power of expressing nice shades of thought and feeling."

Perhaps there may be a question between the English "again rising" and the Latin "resurrection;" but "conscience" is superior to "in-wit," "remorse" to "again-bite;" and what home-bred Englishman could ape the high-Roman fashion of such togated words as "the multitudinous sea incarnadine"?

Again, " mariner " is felt to be poetically better than "sailor" for emotional purposes, and most people would prefer to say, "It was an ancient mariner" rather than " It was an elderly seaman."

Such shrewd perceptions abound in these Essays: and now, before proceeding, I might, with that kind of careless facility so much in vogue with the critics, point out a few slips or a little slovenliness here and there, as when Mr. LOWELL opines that "Chastelard" was ever popular in England, or that Mr. SWINBURNE really owes very much to ROBERT BROWNING, and quite forgets to mention D. G. ROSSETTI, who was his real master.

I might remark upon his curious notion that CLOUGH was, after all, the great poet of the age, and wonder why, in dealing with POPE's artificiality, he should have failed to allude to that one most perfect and extreme case, "The Dying Christian to his Soul;" or, whilst condemning his want of real pathos, should have forgotten such real bursts of passion as occur in "Eloisa to Abelard."

As to Mr. LOWELL's slovenly style, nothing can be more slipshod than the following on DRYDEN :—"He is always imitating—no, that is not the word," etc. ; or, "The always hasty DRYDEN, as I think I have said before," etc. Every critical notice is expected to contain a few specimens of such flippant signs of the critic's superior acumen, and I hope I shall get credit for them; but the real object of such a discourse as this is, after all, "to give the quality of a man's mind, and the amount of his literary performance." To such business I will try to confine myself.

In Mr. LOWELL's mind, the Conservative and Radical elements are mixed in truly statesmanlike proportions.

Capable of that concentrated passion which did much towards sweeping slavery from his own land, and with a certain bitterness and scepticism towards established forms of religion, no one can fail to be reassured and won by the essential sobriety of his qualifying utterances.

Do you think him a Radical? then note how he dwells on that—

"power of the Past over the minds and conduct of men, which alone insures the continuity of national growth, and is the great safeguard of power and progress ; "

Or again,

"The older Government is the better, and suits ;
New ones hunt folks' corns out like new boots."

His impatience with the sects is with their forms only and their attempts to imprison the Eagle of Faith in the iron cage of Dogma. He quotes with approval SELDEN, who says—

" It is a vain thing to talk of an heretic—a man, for his heart, cannot think any otherwise than he does think ; "

and we can hardly be grateful enough to him for reminding the children of this generation that—

" So soon as an early conviction has cooled into a phrase, its work is over, and the best that can be done with it is to bury it."

But there is one clear note running through the whole of his utterances which makes them fresh as with the sea air.

It is the note of moral supremacy :

" That Moral Supremacy is the only one that leaves monuments and not ruins behind it "—that " great motors of the race are moral, not intellectual, and their force lies ready to the use of the poorest and the weakest of us all ; " that " no man without intense faith in something can ever be in earnest ; " that in *act* a right ambition is to be " a man amongst men, not a humbug amongst humbugs," and in *word* " to give the true coin of speech, never the highly ornamental promise to pay— token of insolvency."

It is not safe to divide Mr. LOWELL's Essays into the heavy and the light, for there come to him flashes of delicate humour in his gravest moods, and he will anon stop and moralize, like THACKERAY, in front of a clown.

Safer is it to separate the volumes roughly into contemporary and non-contemporary.

" Among my Books," 2 vols., are entirely non-contemporary, and full of grave and weighty matter concerning " New England Two Centuries Ago," DRYDEN, SHAKESPEARE, LESSING, ROUSSEAU, DANTE, SPENSER, WORDSWORTH, MILTON, and KEATS.

" My Study Windows," with the exception of " Pope," " Chaucer," and " Notes on the Library of Old Authors," deal entirely with contemporary matters. Such are " My

Garden Acquaintance," "A Good Word for Winter," "On a certain Condescension in Foreigners," "A Great Public Character," whose interest for us begins and ends with this sketch of him—a remark which applies equally, if not more, to "The Life and Letters of JAMES GATES PERCIVAL."

Finally, I may cite an extremely interesting and entertaining section of critical and biographical studies on CARLYLE, ABRAHAM LINCOLN, THOREAU.

To this last I will add a notice of EDGAR POE's life and works, written at his own request in 1845, and attached to an edition of POE's works in 4 vols.

No true American can touch upon the early settlement of the Pilgrim Fathers upon the barren coast of Massachusetts, and the momentous national life which grew out of it, without an irrepressible glow of feeling.

It is like the sentiments of the Swiss about WILLIAM TELL. Mr. LOWELL's "New England Two Centuries Ago" is a prose idyll of suppressed poetical fervour.

He calls the history "dry and unpicturesque." "There is no rustle of silks, no waving of plumes, no chink of golden spurs," but we soon feel that "the home-spun fates of Cephas and Prudence" have the living interest of life in the catacombs about them, and are "intrinsically poetic and noble." "The noise of the axe, hammer, and saw" rings through it all, and is the physical image of that mighty impulse which drove the Puritan to make "the law of man a living counterpart of the law of God."

This coming out into the wilderness for the sake of an idea is full of a moral chivalry irresistibly attractive to an age bird-limed with the "expedient," and suffocated with the "practical."

It is the indescribable magnet which draws the imagination of sceptical France after a VICTOR HUGO, or the *dolce far niente* of Italy after a GARIBALDI.

Sublime singleness of purpose—divine simplicity of heart
—the little child is again set in the midst of us by the dear
Lord, and presently he overcomes the mailed Goliath with
a sling and a stone !

"Dry and unpoetic," repeats LOWELL, with his great
heart all on fire; "everything is near, authentic, petty,"
"no mist of distance to soften outlines, no image of tra-
dition," only this—that Jehovah, who had become "I was,"
became again "I am" to the Puritans. Yet, were they not
fanatics?—enthusiasts they were ; but work and "business"
saved the balance of character: their very narrowness and
despotism were sensible and judicious.

"They knew that liberty in the hands of feeble-minded men, when
no thorough mental training has developed the understanding and given
the judgment its needful means of comparison and correction," meant
nothing more than "the supremacy of their particular form of imbecility,
a Bedlam chaos of monomaniacs and bores."

The New Englander was without humour, but that
quality has since been largely developed in his descendants,
who fail not to see that Puritanism had an intensely humorous side.

Mr. LOWELL, in the midst of his close sobriety of treatment, has a winning perception of those lighter shades of
the comic which crop up in such a "Miles Gloriosus" as
Captain Underhill, who took up certain heretical opinions
"with all the ardour of personal interest" "on the effi-
ciency of grace without reference to works." His chief
accuser, although he denied the charge of heresy on that
score, was "a sober woman whom he had seduced in the
ship and drawn to his opinion, but who was afterwards
better informed." He told her that he had continued "in
a legal way and under a spirit of bondage," and could get
no "assurance," for about five years, till at length, "as he

was taking a pipe of the good creature tobacco, the Spirit fell upon his heart, an absolute promise of free grace, which he had never doubted, whatsoever sin he should fall into." "A good preparative," adds the chronicler, "for such motions as he familiarly used to make to some of that sex. The next day he was called again and banished," etc. His subsequent grave complaints—claims for promotion in the colony, and profound consciousness of personal merit—are very diverting, especially at the end, where he throws in a neat touch of piety: '"and if the honoured court shall vouchsafe to make some addition, that which hath not been deserved by the same power of God may be in due season."

Here and there a fugitive trace of that simple old life of the early colonists still survives, and with it we must take farewell of them. The picture is caught and crayoned with the quick and tender touch of a poet's pencil :

"Passing through Massachusetts, perhaps at a distance from any house, it may be in the midst of a piece of wood and where four roads meet, one may sometimes even yet see a small, square, one-story building, whose use would not long be doubtful. It is summer, and the flickering shadows of forest leaves dapple the roof of the little porch, whose door stands wide, and shows, hanging on either hand, rows of straw hats and bonnets that look as if they had done good service. As you pass the open window, you hear whole platoons of high-pitched voices discharging words of two or three syllables, with wonderful precision and unanimity. . . . Now, this little building and others like it were an original kind of fortification, invented by the founders of New England. . . . They are the Martello towers that protect our coast. . . . The great discovery of the Puritan fathers was that knowledge was not an alms or pittance . . . but a sacred debt which the commonwealth owed to every one of her children."

Passing from the New England of America to the old England of SHAKESPEARE, we have to note SHAKESPEARE'S good fortune in living at a time when Old England was passing into the new England of modern Europe ; and the reflection, although not new, is well put by Mr. LOWELL when he notes that, had SHAKESPEARE been born fifty years earlier, he would have been damped by a book language not flexible, not popular, not rich, not subdued by practice to definite accentuation; or fifty years later he would have missed the Normanly refined and Saxonly sagacious England of Elizabeth, and found an England absorbed and angry with the solution of political and religious problems.

Mr. LOWELL, like every other thoughtful writer, must have his say on the distinction between genius and originality—and he says it pithily and well :

" Talent sticks fast to the earth. Genius claims kindred with the very workings of nature, so that a sunset shall seem like a quotation from Dante or Milton; and if Shakespeare be read in the very presence of the sea itself, his verse shall but seem nobler for the sublime criticism of ocean."

And how prettily said is this—

" What is the reason that all children are geniuses (though they contrive so soon to outgrow that dangerous quality), except that they never cross-examine themselves on the subject. The moment that process begins, their speech loses its gift of unexpectedness, and they become as tediously impertinent as the rest of us."

And again—

" Genius is a simple thing of itself, however much of a marvel it may be to other men."

Of the endless twaddle about Originality our author makes as short work as does Mr. EMERSON, and very much in that prophet's own spirit :

" Originality is the power of digesting and assimilating thoughts, so that they become parts of our own life."

Or elsewhere :

" Originality consists quite as much in the power of using to purpose what it finds ready to hand as in that of producing what is absolutely new."

Compare this with EMERSON, who points out that SHAKE-
SPEARE was little solicitous whence his thoughts were
derived, and adds—

"Chaucer was a huge borrower," but both "steal by apology—that
which they take has no worth where they find it, and the greatest where
they leave it. . . . It has come to be practically a sort of rule in
literature that a man having once shown himself capable of original
writing is entitled thenceforth to steal from the writings of others at
discretion. Thought is the property of him who can entertain it, and
of him who can adequately place it. A certain awkwardness marks
the use of borrowed thoughts, but as soon as we have learned what to
do with them they become our own."

"SHAKESPEARE once more!" Mr. LOWELL calls his
essay. Does he say anything new? The reader who has
read all that has been written about SHAKESPEARE is the
best judge of that. I have no such pretensions; but the
summing-up on various counts is very good and clear,
especially the remarks on HEMINGE and CONDELL—

"The two obscure actors to whom we owe the preservation of several
of his plays and the famous Folio edition of 1623."

Mr. LOWELL is of opinion that indifferent is the best
extant version as to accuracy; that the rugged, incomplete,
obscure, and irregular passages are all imperfect, and that
SHAKESPEARE never wrote bad metre, rugged rhyme nor
loose and obscure English.

This may be true; at all events, no one can say that it is
not so.

To me it appears like saying that HANDEL never wrote
indifferent music, or that RAFFAELLE is never out of
drawing.

It always seems to me to be putting an ideal strain upon
human nature—this steady elimination of the "pot-boiling"
element. It may not always have been so prominent as in
the case of HANDEL, or poor MORLAND, or FIELDING, or

the divine MOZART ; but one who, like SHAKESPEARE, must have produced with great speed at high pressure, and who certainly was not above writing down to his public, may have occasionally had such a moderate opinion of his audience, and such an indisposition to do the *plus quam satis*, as to leave a passage rough on occasion without much injury to himself or to posterity.

But here am I emptying my little basket on the mighty rubbish-heap of Shakespearian speculation ! Let me rather note Mr. LOWELL's fine appreciation of the way in which at first every one feels himself on a level with this great impersonal personality—how ALPHONSO OF CASTILE fancies he could advise him—how another could tell him there was never a seaport in Bohemia.

" Scarce one (for a century or more after his death) but could speak with condescending approval of that prodigious intelligence, so utterly without compare that our baffled language must coin an adjective—Shakespearian—to qualify it."

And then, as time goes on, every one seems to get afraid of him in turn.

VOLTAIRE plays the gentleman usher—but when he perceives that his countrymen are really seized, turns round upon the placid Immortal and rails at him with his cowardly " Sauvage ivre, sans la moindre étincelle de bon goût ! "

Even GOETHE, who tries to write like him in "Götz" and fails, comes to the conclusion that SHAKESPEARE is no dramatist ; and CHATEAUBRIAND thinks that he has corrupted art.

" He invented nothing," says Lowell, "but seems rather to rediscover the world about him."

Mr. LOWELL's view of " Hamlet " will be specially interesting to Mr. IRVING and his admirers—the more so because Mr. IRVING seems to have come to the same conclusion.

" Is Hamlet mad? " " High medical authority has pronounced, as usual, on both sides of the question " but no—Hamlet is not mad intellectually, he is a psychologist and metaphysician, a close observer both of others and of himself, " letting fall his little drops of acid irony on all who come near him, to make them show what they are made of."

Hamlet deprived of reason is a subject for Bedlam—not for the stage.

If Hamlet is irresponsible, the play is chaos; besides, the feigned madness of Hamlet is one of the few points in which it has kept close to the old story.

Morally, Hamlet drifts through the whole tragedy, never keeping on one tack; feigned madness gives to the inde-cision of his character the relief of seeming to do something, in order as long as possible to escape the dreaded necessity of doing anything at all.

He discourses of suicide, but he does not kill himself—he talks of daggers, uses none—goes to England to get farther from present duty—he is irresolute from over-power of thought.

He is an ingrained sceptic—doubts the soul, even after the ghost scene—doubts Horatio, doubts Ophelia—his cha-racter is somewhat feminine :—but here I break off, in despair of being able to give even a rough idea of Mr. LOWELL'S Hamlet—it is by far the finest piece of literary criticism in the book, and must be studied book in hand ——at the Lyceum.

I here sum up with SHAKESPEARE'S moral—

" Lear may teach us to draw the line more clearly between a wise generosity and loose-handed weakness of giving ; Macbeth, how one sin involved another and for ever another by a fatal parthenogenesis, and that the key which unlocks forbidden doors to our will or passion leaves a stain on the hand that may not be so dark as blood, but that will not out; Hamlet, that all the noblest gifts of mind slip through the grasp of infirm purpose."

I turn the closing pages of this essay, unquoted, with reluctance, and pass to two essays which should be hung like pendant pictures "in every gentleman's library,"— LESSING and ROUSSEAU.

To begin an elaborate essay on LESSING with a disquisition on BURNS is characteristic of an author who prefaces a brief notice of POE with instances of some dozen poets who gave small early promise, as a contrast to POE, who gave great early promise of ability.

After about seven pages, we at last reach LESSING; the seven preceding pages show the extent and carefulness of Mr. LOWELL'S studies at Dresden; of the definite opinions he formed of GOETHE, "limpidly perfect in his shorter poems—failing in coherence in his longer works;" of the Grand Duke, with his whole court in a sensational livery of blue, yellow, and leather breeches, but still capable of manly friendships with GOETHE and HERDER, whose only decoration was genius; of HEINE, who could be daintily light even in German; of German love-making, which he explains to be "a judicious mixture of sensibility and sausages."

However, LESSING is at last seized in the midst of a "setting" a little laboured, with great firmness, and Mr. LOWELL shows his essential gift, commenting with due appreciation on HERR STAHR's life of LESSING, while leaving on the literary easel a portrait of LESSING very unlike HERR STAHR's.

It is in all those points where LESSING differs most from ROUSSEAU, that LESSING charms Mr. LOWELL.

His character was more interesting than his work—she

was lover of truth first and of literature afterwards; his struggles with poverty brought out his native manliness, his genuineness saved him from that fritter, haste, and vapidity which are the snare of book-makers.

When he wants to earn a penny, he says, "I am unhappy, if it must be by writing." "To call down fire from heaven to keep the pot boiling" is no doubt the prophet's bitterest pill—but we are comforted when we think of the many noble works in art and literature which the world would never have had "but for the whips and scourges" of necessity.

In truth, few writers have not discovered that, although inspiration will not always come when called for, it will not often come if it be never called.

EMERSON'S "laying siege to the oracle" is not a bad plan.

"Nothing comes of being long in a place one likes," strikes the key-note of that "restless mounting-upward" endeavour that makes LESSING so congenial a subject to our author.

To LESSING, and not to WIELAND, is traced that revolt from pseudo-classicism in poetry, prelude to the romanticism which ran wild in France in the next century.

In 1767 LESSING was working at the "Laocoön," and in 1758 "Emelia Galotti" was begun; and in 1779 "Nathan the Wise," by which he was chiefly known outside Germany, was published.

In 1781 LESSING died. He may almost be said to have invented German style, and to have converted criticism from the science of party spirit to the service of simplicity and truth.

The greatest critic of his age, he also was the first to see that—

"criticism," as Mr. LOWELL says, "can at best teach writers without genius what is to be avoided or imitated. It cannot communicate life, and its effect, when reduced to rule, has commonly been to produce that correctness which is so praiseworthy—and so intolerable."

That " so intolerable " is quite in M. RENAN's best manner.

Mr. LOWELL's candour and breadth are happily displayed in his remarks upon the sentimentalist ROUSSEAU.

He dislikes him.

His half-conscious hypocrisy, his false sentiment, his self-indulgence and want of true moral fibre, are exactly what are most sickening to his reviewer.

Yet will he not suffer him to be pommelled by BURKE—nay, Irish EDMUND is called "a snob;" but then ROUSSEAU, with all his faults, was a good red-republican, and Mr. BURKE was a person of royalist proclivities.

Neither is old Dr. JOHNSON allowed to jump upon the blithe author of " Emile;" he is promptly reminded of his own friend, "that wretchedest of lewd fellows, RICHARD SAVAGE,"—which is a little hard upon JOHNSON, as RICHARD SAVAGE by no means so adequately represented the *noscitur a sociis* of JOHNSON's mature life, as did " Emile " or the " Confessions " the settled views and tastes of JEAN-JACQUES.

ROUSSEAU is used, perhaps, a little stringently, to " cheapen " BYRON and MOORE.

In comparison with such pet aversions of his, Mr. LOWELL evidently considers JEAN-JACQUES a man of parts and principles.

On the whole, the essay seems very fair to JEAN-JACQUES, and certainly contains some of Mr. LOWELL's finest and most sensitive paragraphs.

" There is nothing so true, so sincere, so downright and forthright as genius; it is always truer than the man himself is—greater than he."

And how well is the trenchant line drawn between poetical and moral sentiment.

" Every man feels instinctively that all the beautiful sentiments in the world weigh less than a single lovely action, and that, while tenderness of feeling and susceptibility to generous emotions are accidents of temperament, goodness is an achievement of the will and a quality of life."

And, further—

" There is no self-delusion more fatal than that which makes the conscience dreamy with the anodyne of lofty sentiments, while the life is grovelling and sensual."

Yet, although ROUSSEAU indulged this self-delusion,

" I cannot help looking on him," writes his American critic, " as one capable beyond any in his generation of being Divinely possessed. . . . The inmost core of his being was religious. . . . Less gifted, he had been less hardly judged. . . . He had the fortitude to follow his logic wherever it led him. . . . More than any other of the sentimentalists, except, possibly, STERNE, he had in him a staple of sincerity. Compared with CHATEAUBRIAND, he is honesty ; compared with LAMARTINE, he is manliness itself."

This last is just a little caustic on a man of whom Mr. LOWELL wrote in 1848,

" This side the Blessed Isles, no tree
Grows green enough to make a wreath for thee ; "

And—

" Only the Future can reach up to lay
The laurel on that lofty nature."

But times change ; so do men and their opinions. Has not Mr. EMERSON, in one of his Olympic moods, declared that—

" Consistency is the bugbear of little minds " ?

and has not Mr. LOWELL analogued the thought in—

" The foolish and the dead alone never change their opinions " ?

In the bright little essay called, " On a Certain Condescension in Foreigners," Mr. LOWELL expresses what are possibly the feelings of many Americans when he says—

"It will take England a great while to get over her airs of patronage towards us, or even possibly to conceal them."

The whole essay is intended, evidently, to be "overheard" on this side of the Atlantic, and is full of humour, wisdom, and wholesome truth, both for Americans and English— especially English. It contains this remarkable political utterance, which could never have been written except by an American, and perhaps by no American but Mr. LOWELL :

"Before the war we were to Europe but a huge mob of adventurers and shopkeepers."

I regret that I cannot dwell at greater length upon the lighter tones of sweet feeling that come streaming in from his "Garden Acquaintance"—like the song of birds in spring, the bobolink and the oriole, the cat-bird and the song-sparrow besides the many birds with which we are familiar in England —all are his friends, and he is their protector.

How sweetly, like SELBORNE or gentle and genial OWEN, does he write—

"If they will not come near enough to me (as most of them will), I bring them down with an opera-glass—a much better weapon than a gun. I would not, if I could, convert them from their pretty pagan ways. The only one I sometimes have savage doubts about is the red squirrel. I *think* he oölogises. I *know* he eats cherries . . . and that he gnaws off the small end of pears to get at the seeds. He steals the corn from under the noses of my poultry. But what would you have? He will come down upon the limb of the tree I am lying under till he is within a yard of me. . . . Can I sign his death-warrant who has tolerated me about his grounds so long? Not I. Let them steal, and welcome. I am sure I should, had I had the same bringing up and the same temptation. As for the birds, I do not believe there is one of them but does more good than harm ; and of how many featherless bipeds can this be said ?"

H

" Elia " himself never beat this in delicacy.

" Winter " is conceived in a similar spirit.

" DRYDEN " and " DANTE " are careful and elaborate studies of the age as well as of the men ; but it is easy to see that Mr. LOWELL'S heart is as much in DANTE as it is out of DRYDEN.

" KEATS " is an affectionate tribute.

Mr. LOWELL finds very little new to say about WORDS-WORTH or SPENSER, but his " CHAUCER " is very careful and sympathetic.

The essay on Witchcraft is, strange to say, the least inte-resting to me—perhaps because it is evidently the least congenial to the writer.

The essay on POPE is as much under-friendly as THACK-ERAY'S " POPE " is over-friendly.

I regret to have no space for comment on the suggestive notice of " President LINCOLN," full of personal insight and true American patriotism. But what we must call the attack on CARLYLE and the panegyric on EMERSON shall wind up this part of my subject.

CARLYLE and EMERSON are most dissimilar : alike in this only, that each has performed the same office for different types of mind in the same century ; both have taught men to think for themselves—CARLYLE by his analysis of the external, EMERSON by his analysis of the internal world.

The one deals with matter in its effect on mind, the other with mind in its effect on matter.

He who is taught by EMERSON is seldom found at the feet of CARLYLE ; and it is strange but true that the readers of CARLYLE have often an antipathy for EMERSON'S style, and most Emersonians detest CARLYLE.

The key of Mr. LOWELL's view of CARLYLE is to be found, of course, in CARLYLE's devotion, and Mr. LOWELL's aversion, to the majesty of physical force.

CARLYLE is the Despot, Mr. LOWELL the Republican, and from his hostile camp he examines the peculiarities of the "Sturm and Drang" school, and separates between the early and the late CARLYLE with a firmness of touch and a plainness of speech which we in England are still afraid to use towards the late venerable sage of Chelsea.

"In the earlier part of his literary career Mr. Carlyle was the denouncer of sham, the preacher-up of sincerity, manliness, and of a living faith. He had intense convictions, and he made disciples. If not a profound thinker, he felt profoundly."

He is represented as a man who hoped great things of humanity; then, later on, grew impatient when disappointed, and ended by hoping nothing of human nature except what could be got out of it by incessant driving and thrashing.

"His latest theory of divine government seems to be the cudgel." He is the "volunteer laureate of the rod." The world for him "is created and directed by a divine Dr. BUSBY."

It would be difficult for Mr. CARLYLE's admirers to rebut this charge, but some of them might point to the obvious fact that the divine government, as we see it to be, *has* this severe, compulsory, and inexorable side to it. It *is* the Government of the Rod, though not of the rod only. Men are compelled and punished into the paths of rectitude and virtue by what we call the laws of nature.

Our GOD is a Divine Despot, and the human despot, when good and wise, is a reflection of at least one side of a divine character.

What Mr. Carlyle scorns and leaves out is the possibility of that free slow development of the individual which is to make him a moral agent in the great scheme—the willing and joyful servitor of the Divine Despot.

Because man will not do right, he must be compelled ; that is pure Carlylese.

But because to do right is in accordance with his own happiness as well as being the will of the Heavenly Despot, therefore his tender training as a free agent to do right freely, and not the "dumb-driven-cattle theory," should be the special and patient care of his earthly ruler—and this, in Mr. LOWELL'S opinion, of course, is a thing better done by a republican than by a monarchical or imperial form of government.

Mr. LOWELL, though he weeps over the prophet of Chelsea, is generously alive to his literary greatness.

"With all deductions, CARLYLE remains the profoundest critic and the most dramatic imagination of modern times."

And again :

"As a purifier of the sources whence our intellectual inspiration is drawn, his influence has been second only to that of WORDSWORTH— if even to his."

There is something much more living and personal about Mr. LOWELL'S account of EMERSON : that great magician, who seemed to dispense so naturally with the definite props of rule and doctrine so essential to most men, because he felt himself so inseparably wedded to the eternal harmonies as never to feel any of them external to himself—that sweet and lofty prophet, who, with piercing yet indulgent eye—

"Above all pain, yet pitying all distress,"

tells us what we know, and gives us the possession of ourselves—that equable temperament, that cloudless serenity whose calm is infectious, and whose deep peace puts everything into proportion.

Though personally Mr. LOWELL prefers a temple (unlike those vast Mexican mysteries of architecture) with a door left for the god to come in—yet he knows that the root of the matter is in EMERSON, who is never out of the presence of the "OVERSOUL," and whose one temple is the round world and the overarching heaven.

To be conformable to eternal law is to be religious—to be natural on the plane of a high and pure nature—to be radiant with the original righteousness which draws the love and reverence of humankind and makes life adorable, instead of for ever struggling with the nightmare of original sin.

This, if anything, is to be prophetic.

This, in spite of what EMERSON calls "the dear old devil," is the witness to the world that "GOD has breathed into man's nostrils the breath of life, and man has become a living soul."

"What an antiseptic is a pure life!" exclaims one who has watched and reverenced EMERSON from boyhood. "At sixty-five, he had that privilege of soul which abolishes the calendar, and presents him to us always the unwonted contemporary of his own prime; . . . we who have known him so long, wonder at the tenacity with which he maintains himself in the outposts of youth."

The brief essay from which I read these words is little more than a warm tribute to Mr. EMERSON as a lecturer.

We are told that as long as he lectured he was an unfailing "draw" in America; but we are told something else—that he was a consummate master of the lecture-art.

Will our eminent men ever, as a rule, think it worth while to acquire this art?—Not so long as £10 is considered an adequate fee for the best lecture, whilst £50 or £100 is willingly given for the best song.

The old country is far behind the new in its estimation of high-class scientific and literary merit.

Platform lecturing is an art like any other; and England will never get good lecturers till she pays for them.

Pray, what sort of fiddling can you get for nothing? LOWELL's essay on EMERSON is—what I hope these two lectures here rolled into one on LOWELL will prove to be— a way of referring readers to the fountain-head, more than an analysis of the waters that flow from it.

Personally, like so many others, to EMERSON I owe my freedom and emancipation from those Stocks of prejudice and those Pillories of public opinion which still make many sit in the world of thought like frightened criminals unable or afraid to stir.

When I was at college I exchanged four handsome volumes of MONTAIGNE for one volume of EMERSON's Essays. I have never regretted my bargain; and when I open my well-worn copy, I still find the Pantheon and the Forest Primeval alike instinct with the great OVERSOUL, and vocal with the music of GOD.

But Mr. LOWELL is a poet.

To many readers he is nothing but a poet, to most nothing but the poet of the " Biglow Papers."

Yet is he as voluminous and many-sided in poetry as in prose ; " he sings to one clear harp in divers tones."

You will have already perceived how impossible it is to treat Mr. LOWELL as a mere, or even as chiefly a humorist —almost as impossible as to leave him out of the list of the chief American humorists.

Indeed, without something like a complete survey, how- ever sketchy, his humour seems hardly to be " placed." It is so imbedded in his life work.

I do not wish to resemble the undergraduate who, in

order to explain the "common pump," began with the "binomial theorem"; but having gone so far into Mr. LOWELL'S prose works, in order to surprise the flashes of his wit and humour, I feel I must now glance at his earlier poems and mark their serious drift, before introducing you to that torrent of merciless wit poured forth in the "Biglow Papers," which, in its intense earnestness and scathing satire, is perhaps the most serious thing in Mr. LOWELL'S life, as it certainly was the most serious service which probably any one writer ever rendered to his country at a great political crisis.

It may be worth while first to sweep away a few critical cobwebs of a general nature.

Silly people are never tired of asking silly questions, which, however, it is not always silly to answer, such as—

Does Mr. LOWELL write like other people?

Yes, and unlike other people too.

Does he copy, imitate, plagiarize?

By all means, and a good deal more besides.

Well, and what does it matter if his early poems flash at times with a certain sympathetic lustre? BEETHOVEN wrote like MOZART, and MOZART like HAYDN, and KEATS, we are told on the best authority, wrote like the authors he happened to be reading.

When LOWELL writes—

> "Wise with the history of its own frail heart,
>   With reverence and sorrow, and with love,"

we seem to hear WORDSWORTH; and the lady Rosaline of whom he declares—

> "Thou look'dst on me all yesternight :
>   Thine eyes were blue, thy hair was bright," etc.,

did not live a hundred miles from "Oriana," "Mariana,"
· *et id omne genus.*

Is not BRYANT's delicate love of the woods in "The
Oak" and the "Birch Tree?" does not SCOTT sing in "Sir
Launfal"? and mark, dear Snail, before you enter your
flowerpot, the most curious rings of MOORE and POE mixed
up together in—

> "O my life, have we not had seasons
>   That only said, live and rejoice !
> That asked not for causes and reasons,
>   But made us all feeling and voice ;
>
> "When we went with the winds in their blowing,
>   When nature and we were peers,
> And we seemed to share in the flowing
>   Of the inexhaustible years ?
>
> " Have we not from the earth drawn juices
>   Too fine for earth's sordid uses?
>   Have I heard—have I seen
>   All I feel and I know ?
>   Doth my heart overween ?
>   Or could it have been
>   Long ago?"

And Echo seems to answer—

> "Ulalume ! Ulalume !"

The unhappy lot of Mr. KNOTT, with its—

> "Meanwhile the cats set up a squall,
>   And safe upon the garden wall
>   All night kept cat-a-walling,"

is quite *à la* HOOD, is it not? and "An Ember Picture" is
quite *à la* LONGFELLOW.

Every poet abounds in similar phenomena; if, for instance, GEORGE HERBERT writes—

> " *Immortal Love*, author of this great frame,
>   Sprung from that beauty which can never fade,

> How hath man parcelled out thy glorious name
> And thrown it on the *dust which thou hast made ?*"

And Tennyson writes—

> "Strong Son of God, *Immortal love*
>
> Thou madest death, and lo ! thy foot
> Is on the skull *which thou hast made*,"

put in thy horns, O Snail, but otherwise no one is much moved by the striking coincidence, and Mr. LOWELL is the last person, as we shall notice by-and-by, to scorn or deny the tributaries which have washed down their many golden sands into his bright lake.

. It is also tolerably idle to inquire whether Mr. LOWELL is more of a poet than a teacher, or more of a teacher than a poet. "Here's LOWELL," he writes anonymously of himself—

> " . . who's striving Parnassus to climb
> With a whole bale of *isms* tied together with rhyme ;
> The top of the hill he will ne'er come nigh reaching
> Till he learns the distinction 'twixt singing and preaching."

He never learnt it—he never seriously meant to learn it.

Song, satire, and parable—more and more as he lives and ponders and pours forth—are all so many pulpit illustrations or platform pleas.

But the world calls him poet, and thereby confers upon him a higher kind of excellency than any ambassadorial rank. And the world is right. The *key-note* is struck early in the poems ranging from 1839–49.

"The leading characteristics of an author who is in any sense original . . . may commonly be traced more or less clearly in his early works."

And what he further says of Carlyle is also true of himself, for in his earliest writings—

"We find some not obscure hints of the future man."

The deep *religious instinct* emancipated from all forms, but vibrating with the fitful uncertainty of an Æolian harp to "the wind which bloweth where it listeth," this is the first thing in LOWELL's mind, as it is the second in LONGFELLOW's, and the third in BRYANT's :

> " There is no broken reed so poor and base,
> No rush the bending tilt of swamp-fly blue
> But He therewith the ravening wolf can chase
> And guide His flock to springs and pastures new ;
> Through ways unlooked for and through many lands,
> Far from the rich folds built with human hands,
> The gracious footprints of His love I trace."

In harmony with which wider prospects the Bible-thumber is aptly rebuked :

> "Slowly the Bible of the race is writ,
> And not on paper leaves nor leaves of stone :
> Each age, each kindred, adds a verse to it,
> Texts of despair or hope, of joy or moan."

And next to this deep *love of God,* of which more hereafter, is our poet's *love of man.* It is the love of the man in all men, of the womanly in every woman—the true enthusiasm of humanity—which—

> " Sees beneath the foulest faces lurking
> One God-built shrine of reverence and love."

Further in harmony with which essential humanity, his pity for the frail and erring is characteristically edged with the fiercest scorn :

> " Thou wilt not let her wash thy dainty feet
> With such salt things as tears, or with rude hair
> Dry them, soft Pharisee, that sitt'st at meat

> With Him who made her such, and speak'st Him fair,
> Leaving God's wandering lamb the while to bleat
> Unheeded, shivering in the pitiless air."

With the clear-headed young poet, a man already counts only for one, and every one to be weighed in the same balance.

BURNS'S " A man's a man for a' that " often rings in our ears—it flashes out in " Where is the true man's Fatherland?" and broadens at length into that long magnificent and victorious cry for freedom which rings like a clarion high above all other voices throughout the remainder of LOWELL'S works.

This note once firmly struck, all further trifling is at an an end. He may have sung with a Tennysonian ring:

> " . . . On Life's lonely sea,
> Heareth the marinere
> Voices sad, from far and near,
> Ever singing full of fear,
> Ever singing drearfully."

But this spirit once touched by—

> " That sunrise whose Memnon is the soul of man,"

he is on his way attended by a nobler vision of melody than that of any siren from Fairyland:

> " Thou alone seemest good,
> Fair only Thou, O Freedom, whose desire
> Can light in mildest souls quick seeds of fire,
> And strain life's chords to the old heroic mood."

It was a passion rising legitimately out of the love of man—that enthusiasm, that grace so Pauline, so rare. And although the harp is new and the minstrel young, we may well revive such noble preludings as—

> " Men ! whose boast it is that ye
> Come of fathers brave and free,

If there breathe on earth a slave,
Are ye truly free and brave?
If ye do not feel the chain
When it works a brother's pain,
Are ye not base slaves indeed,
Slaves unworthy to be freed?

" Women ! who shall one day bear
Sons to breathe New England air,
If ye hear, without a blush,
Deeds to make the roused blood rush
Like red lava through your veins
For your sisters now in chains—
Answer ! are ye fit to be
Mothers of the brave and free? "

And how pertinent, yet how fanatical and visionary, must some lines have seemed to those who dared not side with truth—

" Ere her cause brought fame and profit, and 'twas prosperous to be just ! "

Listen to the advanced guard of Slavery Abolition :

" They are slaves who fear to speak
For the fallen and the weak ;
They are slaves who will not choose
Hatred, scoffing, and abuse

Rather than in silence shrink
From the truth they needs must think ;
They are slaves who dare not be
In the right with two or three."

Slaves they might be, but in those days to be in the right with two or three meant to be assaulted in public, as was Senator SUMNER by Senator BROOKES in 1856, for speaking against slavery in the House.   It meant to find oneself in the tight boots of those two judges who, in the famous "Dred Scott Case," 1857, stood firm against the five other judges who were for the extradition of a slave captured in a free State.

Yes; and the sort of high thinking and plain speaking which did more than anything else to remedy this state of things, and to blow the liberation spark into a sacred flame, is to be found in such pathetic utterances as—

" The traitor to Humanity is the traitor most accursed ;
Man is more than Constitutions : better rot beneath the sod,
Than be true to Church and State while we are doubly false to God ! "

And again :

" He's true to God who's true to man ; wherever wrong is done
To the humblest and the weakest, 'neath the all beholding sun,
That wrong is also done to us ; and they are slaves most base
Whose love of right is for themselves, and not for all their race."

Never did a man trust himself more unreservedly to the guidance of "a blazing principle "—never did "principle" bring a man through more triumphantly !

As a thinker and a writer, better than as a legislator, LOWELL could afford to be uncompromising in his allegiance to the rights of man, to humanity, to freedom—and he was.

He helped to strengthen by those few early flights of song the hands of the actors, and to comfort the hearts of the people.

He was one of the first to feel and to cry aloud that—

" Still is need of martyrs and apostles ! "

And those typical lines, not against slavery only, but against the Mexican war in the crisis of 1845, are amongst the noblest and broadest of all his verses :

" For mankind are one in spirit, and an instinct bears along,
Round the earth's electric circle, the swift flash of right or wrong ;
Whether conscious or unconscious, yet Humanity's vast frame
Through its ocean-sundered fibres feels the gush of joy or shame ;—
In the gain or loss of one race all the rest have equal claim.

   .   .   .   .

Hast thou chosen, O my people, on whose party thou shalt stand,
Ere the Doom from its worn sandals shakes the dust against our land?
Though the cause of Evil prosper, yet 'tis Truth alone is strong."

And further on :

" Truth for ever on the scaffold, Wrong for ever on the throne :
Yet that scaffold sways the future, and behind the dim unknown
Standeth God within the shadow, keeping watch above His own."

But, alas ! of exhortation and invective the world seemed weary. Men soon discovered that shams could do the one and fanatics the other.

Mr. Lowell retired into his armoury, looked at his revolver, his blunderbuss, his broad-sword hanging over the mantelpiece, thought how he had let his barrels off one after another, and how sturdily he had laid about him.

Then he got somewhat tired, wondered why he had not done more execution, why the people did not read and buy more.

Presently a long, thin stiletto caught his eye.

It glittered in a neglected corner ; it had, indeed, never been known to fail in his hands, but had seldom been used.

One merit it possessed—it never rusted, it was always ready.

Its name was " Wit."

Whilst Beecher fulminated with his anti-slavery speeches, and Mrs. Stowe romanced in " Uncle Tom's Cabin," Lowell betook himself year after year to poke up the Constitution in the ribs with that incomparable series of " digs " so widely known as the " Biglow Papers."

" I soon found," writes he, "that I held in my hand a weapon, instead of the fencing-stick I had supposed.

From the Mexican War of 1845 to the close of the Great Rebellion in 1865, people looked to the " Biglow Papers " not only as a current expression of the best aspirations of

National America, but as a running commentary and judgment upon prominent events and persons. Nor is it possible to enter into the "Biglow Papers" without a rough, though definite, idea of the ingredients of American character and the course of American history.

The kernel of the United States—

"Is that New England of Massachusetts and Connecticut which the English Puritans built when they only thought to build Zion."

Amidst all subsequent accretions and modifications, there is a Puritan vigour and enthusiasm at the root of the American character that came from those early settlements.

It is possible to talk nonsense about the Pilgrim Fathers of the *Mayflower*, who went across the sea alone in a barque of 180 tons with forty-one souls on board, and who, when they landed, "knew not at night where to have a bit in the morning."

Still, their work and their influence are alike unprecedented, save in the annals of the Hebrew race.

Still, they are the men who discovered, as Mr. J. R. GREEN says, that "the secret of the conquest of the New World lay not in its gold, but simply in labour."

Still, they remain, as Mr. LOWELL remarks, the only people in modern times who went into exile solely for the privilege of worshipping God in their own way; and this latent idealism has passed into the nation.

"To move John Bull, you must make a fulcrum of beef and pudding; an abstract idea will do for Jonathan."

The religion of the Puritans is the religion of America whenever she has time to remember it :

"God made the earth for man, not trade."

Their faith is likely to survive every other ; it is a singularly simple, vital sort of TRINITY, and its three terms are— GOD, MAN, and WORK !

The modern American owns to three commanding dates— the *Mayflower* date, 1620, that formed the people's religion.

The Independence of the United States, 1787, that formed the people's government.

The Restoration of the United States at the close of the Great Rebellion, 1865, which fixed America's position in the world as a great nation, as well able as, or better able than, England to control its vast outlying possessions, and to hold its own against all comers.

In places Mr. LOWELL speaks almost as if he had no country before the war—nor any so long as Victory trembled in the balance—so great, patriotic, and solidifying an influence does he attribute to the decisive Northern conquest.

The " Biglow Papers " cannot be read apart from a close reference to events between 1845 and 1865.

The Mexican War in 1845, which " I consider," he writes, "a national crime," set these witty and wise satires a-going.

In 1848 all Europe was in a blaze of excitement about the French Revolution and the sudden success of LOUIS NAPOLEON.

It was despotic power on the side of white bondage in Europe, just as much as LINCOLN's armies were to be despotic against black bondage in AMERICA ; the only difference being that NAPOLEON's army put down Liberty, and LINCOLN's put down slavery.

To a few sanguine Northerners it seemed, even in 1843, that the—

> " Time was ripe, and rotten ripe, for change :
> Then let it come ; I have no fear of what
> Is called for by the instinct of mankind. "

I know nothing more capricious or inexorable than this same "instinct." It lies dormant; it wakes and goes to sleep again; it is often at the mercy of circumstances, half driven, half led—a most obstinate beast when wanted to move on, and yet at critical moments apt to take the bit between its teeth and rush.

The smart goadings of the "Biglow" diatribes show the progress of the Abolition instinct under patriotic guidance.

KOSSUTH lands in 1851.

"Uncle Tom's Cabin" is published in 1852.

The DUCHESS OF SUTHERLAND adopts an Englishwomen's address signed by 576,000 against slavery in the same year.

In 1859 a good many people think JOHN BROWN a hero for opposing the introduction of slavery into Kansas, and in 1860 the rest hang him.

His soul, however, was generally understood to be "marching on," so much so that ABRAHAM LINCOLN—a notorious anti-slavery man—is elected President in the same year, 1860, and the secession of five slave states followed.

At this moment it was not easy to see clear.

"Biglow" saw quite clear, and was for going fast.

LINCOLN also saw clear, and was for going slow—that is to say, until he had an army to go fast with—then he went very fast.

The Puritan States of Massachusetts and Pennsylvania stood firm from the first.

Then came the momentous years 1861-62, the rise of the great Federal generals M'CLELLAN and SHERMAN, the election of the Southern President, JEFF. DAVIS—and LINCOLN goes fast.

In 1861 he calls for 42,000 volunteers and a loan of 250 millions of dollars, and lets the world know that he means to fight.

I

In 1862 he calls for 300,000 more volunteers, and soon runs up the National Debt (paid off in 1836) to 1,222,000,000 dollars.

This was smart, but the reader of " Biglow " will not fail to note the sensitive sneer at England's neutrality—and the open bitterness at that short-lived European recognition ot the South, rescinded on the failure of the rebellion.

It is perfectly true that here in England we did not know which side would win—and as the slaves were not ours, we did not feel inclined to give the national abolitionists anything but a private moral support.

France did the same, and we both got a thank-you-for-nothing at the end of the war.

I think in England most of us were ot opinion that if the South *could* secede, it was sufficiently distinctive and powerful to take care of itself; otherwise, it was manifestly a rebel.

Slavery was an element in the social life of another people which we abhorred and had abolished in our own, but which we would no more go out of our way to put down on a foreign soil than we should go about to put down capital punishment, the knout, polygamy, or restrictive tariffs abroad.

The independence of the Southern States was or was not a fact ; we treated it as a fact, and we were wrong.

Slavery to us was an external question for internal legislation, but not for our legislation ; we had dealt with it and done with it ; we advised Brother Jonathan to do likewise ; but from the first we meant to stand out of the quarrel just as we did in the Franco-Prussian war (as we ought to have in the Crimean war), and we did stand out of it to such purpose that in 1881 we have the strongest Abolitionist in America as ambassador at the Court of St. James, and if we are to judge by his genial speeches and pleasant bearing amongst us, we have him here in no unfriendly spirit, although he has said some bracing things about us.

In 1862 the time seemed, indeed, "rotten ripe"; LINCOLN suspends the Habeas Corpus Act, and proclaims the Southern slaves free; in 1863 calls for 300,000 more volunteers, and proves by the response how complete is his mastery of the situation.

Meanwhile "Mr. Biglow" is fain to tell us how monstrous peculation and corruption turns up in the army supplies; but the rise of General GRANT is the beginning of the end (not quite the end of corruption, to be sure), and in 1864 M'CLELLAN actually declares for the Union as a bid for the Presidency, and even divides the Democratic party on the question.

But by this time about 2000 battles had been fought; it was clear LINCOLN would not give in; it was clear that he was backed; it was clear that slavery was doomed.

In 1864 LINCOLN was re-elected.

In 1865 the flag of the Union once again floated over Charlestown.

In 1865 JEFF. DAVIS, the Southern President, was captured; slavery was abolished throughout America, and ABRAHAM LINCOLN was shot through the head at LORD's Theatre, dying at 7.15 on April 15th.

Most people in America felt that the great event of the century was over, and the noble success of LINCOLN's life had rendered his brutal assassination politically unimportant.

Other men could finish his work, and they have finished it. The "Biglow Papers" show that work in progress; and are as historically valuable as any State paper connected with the abolition of slavery.

Mr. LOWELL will undoubtedly take rank amongst American writers by them.

In these satires he settles into his work with a will—he has an end, and he knows the means—he is thorough and exhaustive; slavery is looked at all round; not an argument is forgotten.

The Slave is placed.

The Master is placed.

The politician is placed.

He paints at one time with a dab of colour, at another he etches elaborately—but always with the same firmness and certainty of touch, and always with equal deliberation.

There is nothing of the "greased lightning" about his wit : it never plays about his subject, it always riddles it through and through.

Those elaborate prefaces remind me of WALTER SCOTT'S protracted and realistic introductions—there is the same infinite leisure of reality about them, whatever slang or apparent frivolity there may be in the form.

This piercing realism redeems the form; behind the mask is a man terribly in earnest—but not over a crotchet —over a passion which he knows sleeps in the heart of all, and must be aroused,—the love of Freedom.

Trusting himself boldly to the deep and often stifled conscience of the people, he chooses their very dialect.

He has done for the American what BURNS and SCOTT did for the Scotch vernacular—it is a bold experiment, one but half understood in this small island, but one which succeeded perfectly with the public addressed.

Before the "Biglows," few people in England read Mr. LOWELL ; since the "Biglows," few people have ceased to read him.

And what is the plan of the "Biglows"? who are the *dramatis personæ?* and what, in short, are the poems about?

The plan of the "Biglows" is laid out in Prose and Poetry. The most whimsical prefaces, avowedly from the pen of the Rev. Homer Wilbur, introduced the curious metrical exercises of Mr. Hosea Biglow and Mr. Birdofredum Sawin. But the subject-matter was momentous.

"Then there was the danger of vulgarizing deep and sacred convictions" by adopting a light, even comic, form. "I needed," says Mr. LOWELL, "on occasion to rise above the level of mere *patois*, and for this purpose I conceived the Rev. Wilbur, who should express the more cautious element of the New England character and its pedantry ; and Mr. Biglow, who should serve for its homely common sense, vivified and heated by conscience. I invented Mr. Birdofredum Sawin for the close of my little puppet-show."

He represents the "half-conscious immorality" of the period—"the recoil of a gross nature from Puritanism "—he always tries to be on the winning side. He is of opinion that—

> "A ginooine statesman should be on his guard,
>   Ef he *must* hev beliefs, nut to b'lieve 'em tu hard."

He also is of opinion that—

> "The fust thing or sound politicians to larn is,
>   Thet Truth, to dror kindly in all sorts o' harness,
>   Mus' be kep' in the abstract . . ."

The poetical figures are Sawin and Biglow, but the whole show is animated by that great prose writer, the Rev. Homer Wilbur. He touches up their compositions, favours us with his own, and gives that variety of subject, together with a unity of purpose, to the "Biglows" which is one of their greatest charms.

Around the stormy topics of war, slavery, and politics,

plays an incessant summer lightning of literary, antiquarian and instructive social and domestic twitter.

The other characters may be dummies, but the Rev. Wilbur is positively alive—he is as solid and elaborate as Scott's Dominie Samson, and dressed out with the apparently careless, but profound, art of Shakespeare's walking gentlemen.

And then, he is absolutely new. Such a superfluously delightful personage has scarcely been sketched before, and may never be sketched again.

The Rev. Homer Wilbur must not be hurried over—though he is in small type, he is like a postscript which contains the pith of a letter, and embedded in those prolix and tediously amusing notes and prefaces are to be found some of Mr. LOWELL's best thoughts and noblest paragraphs in prose.

We look in at the Rev. Homer Wilbur's at all hours of the day; we like to see the old fellow shuffling about his study, with an absurdly unconscious appreciation of his own importance—with his runic inscriptions, his Latin quotations, his eternal twaddle about the Ptolemies, the Lacedæmonians, St. Anthony of Padua, or Pythagoras.

Then, what more artless than his account of that great epic, in twenty-four books, on the taking of Jericho, "which my wife secreted just as I had arrived beneath the walls, and begun a description of the various horns and their blowers," or his "latest conclusion concerning the tenth horn of the beast;" his relations with his parishioners—his sermons—his innocent vanity—his domestic affairs—his utter inability to see the absolute irrelevance of matter such as—

"We had our first fall of snow on Friday. . . . A singular circumstance occurred in this town on the 20th October, in the family of Deacon Pelatiah Tinkham. On the previous evening, a few moments before prayers, . . ."

Here the editor's patience breaks down, and he prints no more.

Still it is never safe to skip the rev. gentleman's effusions —you are sure to miss something good.

How happy is his definition of speech and speech-making:

"By the first we make ourselves intelligible—by the second, unintelligible;"

Or of Congress—

"A mill for the manufacture of gabble,"

A timely warning to our own House of Commons!

"Nothing," he remarks, "takes longer in saying than anything else."

And we can pardon a good deal about the monk Copres, the Dioscuri, and even Marathon—for the sake of those noble wrestlings and honest flashes of thought and feeling with which, like "the Puritan hug" so much dreaded by "Satan," the Rev. Wilbur meets and throws the Demon of Slavery again and again.

"Thor was the strongest of the gods, but he could not wrestle with Time;"

No more was the abolition spirit of the age to be crushed. How grim and pungent is—

"Providence made a sandwich of Ham to be devoured by the Caucasian race"!

And again—

"I think that no ship of state was ever freighted with a more veritable Jonah than this same domestic institution of ours [slavery]. Mephistopheles himself could not feign so bitterly, so satirically sad a sight as this of three millions of human beings crushed beyond help or hope by this one mighty argument, *Our fathers knew no better*. Nevertheless, it is the unavoidable destiny of Jonahs to be cast overboard sooner or later."

But the Rev. Wilbur is of course most eloquent and convincing when he is a mere mask for LOWELL himself ; only now and then do we get such a heated flight as this—

"In God's name, let all who hear, nearer and nearer, the hungry moan of the storm and the growl of the breakers, speak out ! But, alas ! we have no right to interfere. If a man pluck an apple of mine, he shall be in danger of the justice ; but if he steal my brother, I must be silent. Who says this? Our Constitution, consecrated by the callous consuetude of sixty years, and grasped in triumphant argument by the left hand of him whose right hand clutched the clotted .slave-whip. Justice, venerable with the undethronable majesty of countless æons, says, SPEAK ! The Past, wise with the sorrows and desolations of ages, from amid her shattered fanes and wolf-housing palaces, echoes, SPEAK ! Nature, through her thousand trumpets of freedom, her stars, her sunrises, her seas, her winds, her cataracts, her mountains blue with cloudy pines, blows jubilant encouragement, and cries, SPEAK ! From the soul's trembling abysses the still small voice not vaguely murmurs, SPEAK ! But, alas ! the Constitution and the Honourable Mr. Bagowind, M.C., say—BE DUMB ! "

The rev. gentleman dies at last at a very advanced age, leaving in his study heaps of MSS., of which only a few sentences find their way into the columns of the *Atlantic Monthly* :

"Beware of simulated feeling; it is hypocrisy's first cousin ; it is especially dangerous to a preacher ; for he who says one day, ' Go to, let me seem to be pathetic,' may be nearer than he thinks to saying, ' Go to, let me seem to be virtuous, or earnest, or under sorrow for sin.' "

"It is unwise to insist on doctrinal points as vital to religion. The Bread of Life is wholesome and sufficing in itself, but gulped down with these kickshaws cooked up by theologians, it is apt to produce an indigestion, nay, even at last an incurable dyspepsia of scepticism."

"When I see a certificate of character with everybody's name to it, I regard it as a letter of introduction from the Devil."

"There seem nowadays to be two sources of literary inspiration—ulness of mind and emptiness of pocket."

" It is the advantage of fame that it is always privileged to take the world by the button," etc., etc.

Passing to the poems—which bristle with personalities already forgotten, and events that are past—we naturally look for the points of universal interest : each poem, almost each verse, grapples with a principle as much alive now as ever.

A recruiting sergeant for the unjust Mexican War in 1846 calls forth these lively reflections from the honest Hosea Biglow :—

> " Wut's the use o' meetin'-goin'
>   Every Sabbath, wet or dry,
> Ef it's right to go amowin'
>   Feller-men like oats an' rye ?
> I dunno but wut it's pooty
>   Trainin' round in bobtail coats,—
> But its curus Christian dooty
>   This 'ere cuttin' folks's throats.
>
>
> " Wy, it's jest ez clear ez figgers,
>   Clear ez one an' one make two,
> Chaps thet make black slaves o' niggers
>   Want to make wite slaves o' you.
>
>
> Laborin' man an' laborin' woman
>   Hev one glory an' one shame,
> Ev'ry thin' thet's done inhuman
>   Injers all on 'em the same."

The Mexican war is now fully elaborated by what the Rev. Wilbur calls —

" The sacred conclave of tagrag-and-bobtail policy in the gracious atmosphere of the grog-shop," a policy which " shuffles Christ into the Apocrypha," and substitutes for the Apostolic " Fishers of men," " Shooters of men ! "

Mexico is glowingly described to the young recruit as—

> " A sort o'
> Canaan, a reg'lar Promised Land flowin' with rum an' water.'

The reality turns out different :

" For one day you'll most die o' thirst, and 'fore the next git drownded.

I've lost one eye, but thet's a loss it's easy to supply
Out o' the glory that I've gut, fer thet is all my eye ! "

For when, indeed,

". . . Somehow, wen we'd fit an' licked, I ollers found the thanks
Gut kin' o' lodged afore they come ez low down ez the ranks."

To this early period, 1847, belong the famous lines which
were quoted in the House of Commons, and first drew
general attention in England to the satire of Mr. Lowell : —

" Parson Wilbur sez *he* never heerd in his life
Thet th' Apostles rigged out in their swaller-tail coats,
An' marched round in front of a drum an' a fife,
To git some on 'em office, an' some on 'em votes ;
But John P.
Robinson he
Sez they didn't know everythin' down in Judee."

It was now time to be down upon the amazing decla-
mation indulged in by the advocates of slavery—and down
upon them Mr. Biglow was, with a truly delightful specimen
from their own "stump " :—

" Sez John C. Calhoun, sez he—
' Human rights haint no more
Right to come on this floor,
No more 'n the man in the moon,' sez he.

" ' 'The North haint no kind o' bisness with nothin',
An' you've no idee how much bother it saves ;

The mass ough' to labor an' we lay on soffies,
Thet's the reason I want to spread Freedom's aree ;

Now, don't go to say I'm the friend of oppression,
But keep all your spare breath fer coolin' your broth,
Fer I ollers hev strove (at least, thet's my impression)
To make cussed free with the rights o' the North.' "

Here is another fine example of hustings talk destined to
captivate a truly sensible pro-slavery elector :—

" Ez to the slaves, there's no confusion,
In *my* idees consarnin' them—
I think they air an Institution,
A sort of—yes, jest so—ahem :
Do *I* own any ? Of my merit
On thet point you yourself may jedge ;
All is, I never drink no sperit,
Nor I haint never signed no pledge.

" Ez to my princerples, I glory
In hevin' nothin' o' the sort ;
I aint a Wig—I aint a Tory—
I'm jest a candidate, in short."

The lashes that Mr. Biglow would fain see taken off the
slave's back he has no difficulty in applying to the unscrupulous editor of a time-serving newspaper. And "The
Pious Editor's Creed " is followed by one of the prettiest
postscripts in elegant prose on the functions and dignity of
the journalistic profession—from the pen, of course, of the
Rev. Wilbur. Sings the pious editor :—

" I du believe in prayer an' praise
To him thet hez the grantin'
O' jobs,—in every thin' thet pays,
But most of all in CANTIN' ;
This doth my cup with marcies fill,
This lays all thought o' sin to rest—
I *don't* believe in princerple,
But O, I *du* in interest

" I du believe wutever trash
'll keep the people in blindness—
Thet we the Mexicuns can thrash
Right inter brotherly kindness,

> Thet bombshells, grape, an' powder 'n' ball
>   Air good-will's strongest magnets;
> Thet peace, to make it stick at all,
>   Must be druv in with bagnets.

> " In short, I firmly du believe
>   In Humbug generally,
> Fer it's a thing thet I perceive
>   To hev a solid vally;
> This heth my faithful shepherd ben,
>   In pasturs sweet heth led me,
> An' this'll keep the people green
>   To feed ez they hev fed me."

Indeed, some Northern editors felt themselves rather in a fix when the States seceded with a live President in the South, and a STONEWALL JACKSON to boot.

> "Don't never prophesy—unless you know,"

seemed about the safest thing; but appearances were too much for Mr. Sawin, and so on the first Confederate successes he went over to the South, under what some called the flag of "Manifest Destiny." He joins the exultant cry of JEFF DAVIS :—

> " We've all o' the ellerments this very hour
>   That make up a first-class self-governing power;
> We've a war, and a debt, and a flag; and ef this
>   Aint to be independent, why, what on airth is?"

He soon gets into quite a Southern " Dizzy" way of looking or not looking things in the face :—

> " Fact is, the less the people know o' what thar' is a-doin',
>   The handier 'tis for gov'ment—sence it hinders trouble brewin'."

And when things begin to get obviously shaky down South, he remarks :—

> " Nex' thing to knowin' you're well off is *not* to know when y'aint,
>   An' ef Jeff says all's goin' wal, who'll venture t' say it aint ? "

In vain, as the Southern cause, that went up like a rocket, begins to come down with the stick, does Mr. Sawin repeat to himself the noble principles of the new secession :—

> " Wut *do's* Secedin' mean, ef 'taint thet nat'rul rights hez riz, 'n'
> Thet wut is mine's my own, but wut's another man's aint his'n ? "

In vain does the same patriot reflect with complacency that although at times we "du miss silver," yet the Southern notes—

> " Go off middlin' wal for drink, when ther's a knife behind 'em."

The game is nearly up, and Birdofredum Sawin will probably come back to the Union without a blush.

But there were stubborn hearts, and stern lips, and stalwart arms up North that had never wavered. The men who denounced every drop of Mexican blood were ready to pour forth their own like water in a righteous cause.

> " Why, law and order, honor, civil right,
> Ef they aint worth it, what is worth a fight ? "

With such downright, honest fellows the shuffling Statesman gets no quarter. They have got down to—

> " The hard granite of God's first idee."

So cries Biglow—

> " . . . wut's the Guv'ment folks about ?
>
> . . . . .
>
> " Conciliate ? it jest means *be kicked*,
>   No metter how they phrase an' tone it ;
> It means thet we're to set down licked,
>   Thet we're poor shotes an' glad to own it !
>
> . . . . .
>
> " More men ! More men ! It's there we fail ;
>   Weak plans grow weaker yit by lengthenin' ;
> Wut use in addin' to the tail,
>   When it's the head's in need o' strengthenin' ? "

And Biglow can do justice to those fine qualities of the Southern rebels that dazzled and misled all Europe for six months :

> " I tell ye one thing we might larn
> From them smart critters, the Seceders,—
> Ef bein' right's the fust consarn,
> The 'fore-the-fust's cast-iron leaders."

The North, if it was to conquer, had to learn from the South—

> " The strain o' bein' in deadly earnest :
> Thet's wut we want—we want to know
> The folks on our side hez the bravery
> To b'lieve ez hard, come weal, come woe,
> In Freedom ez Jeff doos in Slavery."

The old Puritan Ghost, which is none other than J. R. LOWELL himself behind the curtain, is constantly breaking out with the voice of a prophet—

> "O for three weeks of Crommle and the Lord !
>
> Strike soon, sez he, or you'll be deadly ailin,'
> Folks thet's afeard to fail are sure of failin,'
> God hates your sneakin' creturs that believe
> He'll settle things they run away and leave."

Thus in season and out of season, with fears within and fightings and wars without, did Mr. LOWELL never cease to urge his country's standard-bearer up the hill of difficulty, until once more the star-spangled banner floated over a free and united people.

Our own self-complacency more than once receives a wholesome snub, and we have the advantage of seeing ourselves as others see us.

> " I tell ye, England's law, on sea an' land,
> Hez ollers ben, ' *I've gut the heaviest hand.*'

Of all the sarse thet I can call to mind,
England *doos* make the most onpleasant kind :
It's you're the sinner ollers, she's the saint ;
Wut's good 's all English, all thet isn't aint :

She's praised herself ontil she fairly thinks
There aint no light in Natur when she winks ;

She aint like other mortals, thet's a fact :
She never stopped the habus-corpus act.

She don't put down rebellions, lets 'em breed,
An' 's ollers willin' Ireland should secede ;
She's all thet's honest, honnable, an' fair,
An' when the vartoos died they made her heir."

But then those were days full of burning international questions—days of trial, of intense suspense, of overwrought sensitiveness—when every breath of wind seemed full of fate, and ominous messages went to and fro between the Old and New Worlds.

The case fitted into a nutshell : " John, you pretend to be our good brother. You stand by and see the fight. When we are down in the first few rounds, you won't even hold the sponge. You call yourself neutral, that's trying enough—but presently you act as moral bottleholder to our opponent. You recognize JEFF DAVIS—that's worse; and lastly, you go so far as to threaten, when we have enough to do to fight JEFF, without fighting you."

This—if I may presumptuously act as his spokesman— was the situation from Biglow's point of view, and we may well be surprised at the moderation of Biglow under the circumstances :

" It don't seem hardly right, John,
When both my hands wus full,
To stump me to a fight, John,—
Your cousin, tu, John Bull !

Ole Uncle S. sez he, ' I guess
We know it now,' sez he,
' The lion's paw is all the law,
Accordin' to J. B.,
Thet's fit for you an' me ! '

" We own the ocean, tu, John :
You mus' n' take it hard,.
Ef we can't think with you, John,
It's just your own back-yard.
Ole Uncle S. sez he, ' I guess,
Ef *thet's* his claim,' sez he,
' The fencin'-stuff 'll cost enough
To bust up friend J. B.
Ez wal ez you an' me ! '

" Why talk so dreffle big, John,
Of honor, when it meant
You didn't care a fig, John,
But jest for *ten per cent.* ?
Ole Uncle S. sez he, ' I guess
He's like the rest,' sez he ;
' When all is done, it's number one
Thet's nearest to J. B.
Ez wal ez you an' me ! ' "

Nor does this stinging lyric close without the inevitable
latent threat that stamps almost every political utterance of
America in the midst of all her goodwill towards us :

" Shall it be love or hate, John ?
It's you thet's to decide ;
Aint *your* bonds held by Fate, John,
Like all the world's beside ?
Ole Uncle S. sez he, ' I guess
Wise men forgive,' sez he,
' But not forget ; an' some time yet
Thet truth may strike J. B.
Ez wal ez you an' me ! ' "

In the last verse the lingo of the modern work is incomparably mixed with the faith of the old Puritan and the aspirations of the new American :

> " God means to make this land, John,
> Clear thru, from sea to sea,
> Believe an' understand, John,
> The *wuth* o' bein' free.
>   Old Uncle S. sez he, ' I guess
>   God's price is high,' sez he ;
> ' But nothin' else than wut He sells
>   Wears long, an' thet J. B.
>   May larn, like you and me ! ' "

The popularity of the " Biglows " was immediate and wide.

They provided Lincoln with a current political pamphlet on his own side in his <u>own</u> style.

They relieved fearlessly the burdened hearts of a million patriots—they gave to American literature a noble nature and a new humorist.

It seems a pity to omit all descriptive allusion to such considerable poems as "The Cathedral," "A Fable for Critics," not to mention the Odes on Special Occasions, and a variety of other miscellaneous poems, such as those fugitive garlands of song flung to KOSSUTH, LAMARTINE, CHANNING ; or "To the Memory of THOMAS HOOD." But all further allusion must be brief.

" The Cathedral " is Notre Dame de Chartres—it might have been any other. It is the excuse for a local meditation on things human and divine.

Into such modes we all sometimes fall.

They lie grotesquely near to the common ways of life, yet are they like sacred bowers, whose " open sesame " belongs to the latch-key of the soul alone.

K

Ordering dinner at the Peagreen Inn at Chartres, he finds himself in the presence of two Englishmen—

> " Who made me feel, in their engaging way,
>   I was a poacher on their self-preserve."

Presently one attacks what he supposes to be a hostile Gaul of the place :

> " ' Esker vous ate a nabitang ? ' he asked,
>   ' I never ate one ; are they good ? ' asked I."

Then he loiters through the town by himself, and whilst he lingers in front of the old façade, with its two unequally yoked towers, or gazes at the gorgeous windows inside, there come to the poet those snatches of meditation which are interesting as glimpses of that deep religious feeling which I have before alluded to as the real keynote of Mr. LOWELL's mind.

> " ' 'Tis irrecoverable, that ancient faith ! ' "

he exclaims ; but then, if mediæval Christianity is extinct, "if angels go out," it is only, as EMERSON has it, that "the archangels may come in " with the " Christ that is to be."

The 'stars do not alter with the telescope, the central verities shine on, and—

> " Man cannot be God's outlaw if he would."

But the poet's quick eye turns to our modern blot—bondage to the old letter—and he points instinctively in the direction of that East towards which so many eyes are turned, as though they beheld the sky growing bright :

> " Science was Faith once ; Faith were Science now,
>   Would she but lay her bow and arrows by,
>   And arm her with the weapons of the time.
>   Nothing that keeps thought out is safe from thought.

Freedom of inquiry, unfettered spontaneous utterance, free play and exercise of the noblest aspirational impulses, as there has too long been free play and exercise of the basest —such are the deep undertones. Yet, what absence of Iconoclasm, what tenderness for the past !—

> " Where others worship I but look and long ;
> For though not recreant to my fathers' faith,
> Its forms to me are weariness, and most
> That drony vacuum of compulsory prayer,
> Still pumping phrases for the Ineffable,
> Though all the valves of memory gasp and wheeze."

Yet he has his own invocation :

> " O Power, more near my life than life itself
> (Or what seems life to us in sense immured),
> Even as the roots, shut in the darksome earth,
> Share in the tree-tops joyance, and conceive
> Of sunshine and wide air and wingèd things
> By sympathy of nature, so do I ·
> Have evidence of Thee so far above,
> Yet in and of me ! . . .
> I fear not Thy withdrawal."

How many Christian " Apologists " in their hearts can say as much ?

Fear and trembling is in every whine and quaver of the voice, doubt in each deprecating look ; indeed, to hear some sermons, one might almost suppose that the great Author of all was the prisoner at the bar, whilst the man in the pulpit was acting as special pleader in a shaky case.

Apology may be good armour, but it never won a fight nor made a convert.

If you want to win others, you must believe yourself ; and if you want to believe, you must feel ; and if you would feel, you must learn to attend to and trust those—

> " Intimations clear of wider scope,
> Hints of occasion infinite, that keep

> The soul alert with noble discontent,
> And onward yearnings of unstilled desire."

It is glimpses of these—

> " Spacious circles luminous with mind,
> Those visitations fleet,"

that have power to make him smile equally at all attempts
to build up or destroy a faith in God and the soul :

> "I that still pray at morning and at eve !"

No system, no dogma about this, but ever the incom-
municable touch of reality—grave, sober, and with a sort of
old-world restfulness about it, contrasting quaintly enough
with the feverish rapidity and irritable self-consciousness of
modern life.

In his " Fable for Critics," with its fantastic prose preface
in metre, Mr. LOWELL passes in review a procession of contemporary authors, himself amongst them.

Its wit at once hit the public taste.

It held the mirror up to nature in the magazine hack,
whose effusions—

> " Filled up the space nothing else was prepared for,
> And nobody read that which nobody cared for."

And in the classical bore, who—

> " Could gauge the old books by the old set of rules,
> And his old set of nothings pleased very old fools.

Of EMERSON, in the early days, he says :

> " All admire, and yet scarcely six converts he's got
> To I don't (nor they either) exactly know what ;
> For though he builds glorious temples, 'tis odd
> He leaves ne'er a doorway to get in a god.
> 'Tis refreshing to old-fashioned people like me
> To meet such a primitive Pagan as he."

Perhaps it is a little hard to say of BRYANT that—

> " If he stir you at all, it is just, on my soul,
>   Like being stirred up with the very North Pole."

And though his appreciation of LONGFELLOW, WASHING-TON IRVING, and HAWTHORNE is generous, it is rather severe to dub poor POE—

> " Three-fifths of him genius and two-fifths sheer fudge."

But to be smart, funny, and Hood-like seems to be for once the satirist's only ambition in the " Fable for Critics," and whoever reads these contents of a graveyard will say that he has succeeded :

> " There are slave-drivers quietly whipt underground,
>   There bookbinders done up in boards are fast bound ;
>   There card-players wait till the last trump be played ;
>   There all the choice spirits get finally laid.
>   There the babe that's unborn is supplied with a berth ;
>   There men without legs get their six feet of earth ;
>   There lawyers repose, each wrapt up in his case ;
>   There seekers of office are sure of a place ;
>   There defendant and plaintiff get equally cast ;
>   There shoemakers quietly ' stick to the last.'"

The lines—

> " Nature fits all her children with something to do,
>   He who would write and can't write can surely review,"

remind us forcibly of two lines I remember reading, I think, in MOORE :

> " If you do not write verses, why, what can you do ?
>   The deuce is in't, sir, if you cannot review ! "

We have not space to cull the many felicitous lines that deserve to pass into the language, such as :

> " The world's a woman to our shifting mood.
>
>   And only manhood ever makes a man.

The orchards turn to heaps o' rosy cloud.

The green grass floweth like a' stream
    Into the ocean's blue.

"Our seasons have no fixed returns;
    Without our will they come and go;
At noon our sudden summer burns,
    Ere sunset all is snow.

"But each day brings less summer cheer,
    Crimps more our ineffectual spring;
And something earlier every year
    Our singing birds take wing.

"O thou, whose days are yet all spring,
    Faith blighted once is past retrieving;
Experience is a dumb dead thing,
    The victory's in believing!"

Ladies and gentlemen, I think I can do no better than close this estimate of JAMES RUSSELL LOWELL—his literary performance, together with such flashes of personality as leap forth spontaneously from its many-sided facets—with these words of his great friend and master, EMERSON,—words truly applicable to the few men who have measured their own time with temperate eyes; the few workers who have made their own country better and greater; "the few souls that have made our souls wiser": "The world is his who can see through its pretensions. . . . The day is always his who works in it with serenity and great aims. The unstable estimates of men crowd to him whose mind is filled with a trust, as the heaped waves of the Atlantic follow the moon."

IV

ARTEMUS WARD.

IV.

ARTEMUS WARD.

OOR Artemus! I shall not see his like again, as he appeared for a few short weeks before an English audience at the Egyptian Hall, Piccadilly.

Sometimes, as to looks, profoundly dejected, at others shy or reproachful; nervously anxious to please (apparently), yet with a certain twinkle at the back of his eye which convinced you of his perfect *sang froid;* and one thing always—full, unescapably full, of fun.

The humour of Artemus was delicate, evanescent, and personal to an irritating degree. "I have bin troying," said the impetuous Irishman, after hearing Macready, "for an hour to spake it out, loike that man, but, be-gohrra! I cannot at all—at all!" And no one ever yet succeeded in "spaking it out" like Artemus Ward.

Dickens or Sterne or Swift need no author's interpretation.

People rushed to hear Dickens read; for my part, I always preferred reading Dickens.

But much of Artemus Ward is simply flat without Artemus. And yet the dullest man cannot spoil some of his jokes—there is no mistake about them.

Was there ever a wittier motto than the one over his show—

"Ladies and gentlemen! You cannot expect to go in without paying your money, but you can pay your money without going in."

He said of JEFFERSON DAVIS, the Southern President, soon after the collapse of the rebellion :

"It would have been ten dollars in Jeff's pocket if he had never been born."

The Mormons and BRIGHAM YOUNG always excited his fancy; he never comes within sight of the Salt Lake City, or any of its inhabitants, without cutting an involuntary caper.

Of the Mormons generally he remarks—

"Their religion is singular, but their wives are plural."

He is always delightful on BRIGHAM YOUNG.

"BRIGHAM," he remarks, "is an indulgent father and a numerous husband ; he has married two hundred wives ; he loves not wisely but two hundred well. He is dreadfully married," continues the lecturer, "he is the most married man I ever saw. When I was up at Salt Lake City I was introduced to his mother-in-law. I can't exactly tell you how many there is of her, but it's a good deal."

But another class of sayings, the most irresistible and effective of all, are scarcely worth printing.

The mere padding and absolute platitudes in WARD'S lectures were always received with the greatest applause.

When he seemed hard up, utterly without any matter to go on with, and at the same time quite indifferent to the fact of having nothing whatever to say, then he culminated with a certain brazen effrontery perfectly captivating such, as—

"Time passed on. It always does, by the way. You may possibly have noticed that time passes on."

And, not ashamed of sinking to the lowest depth of impudent dulness, he added, with the greatest conceivable *gusto—*

"It is a kind of way time has."

No one can render this, any more than his famous allusion to Newgate. Describing the overland mail coach as "a den on wheels," in which he had been packed for ten days and nights, he continued—

"Those of you who have been in Newgate——"

The roars which here interrupted the impassive lecture r seemed for a moment to shake his equanimity. He looked like a man abashed and shocked at the breach of taste into which he had been betrayed ; but, feeling all the time that the fatal words could not be recalled, he continued calmly—

"And stayed there any length of time—as visitors, I mean——"

.These bursts of quaint humour could only live at all in that subtle atmosphere which ARTEMUS WARD'S presence created, and in which he alone was able to operate.

His public in about five minutes responded to the slightest breath and brain wave.

The original and genial master who stood before them, demure, impassive, quite simple, unaffected, and a little *gauche,* twiddling his riding-whip or small cane, in reality played upon that audience like an old fiddle.

People laughed before the jokes were out of his lips.

I have heard many orators and seen many actors, but I never saw such a perfect case of magnetic control.

Yet some of his hearers were always left out in the cold— not many, but a few faces remained grave, indignant, like people who had been hoaxed and wanted their money back.

They never smiled, whilst the tears streamed down their

neighbours' cheeks : they came away, saying they could see nothing in ARTEMUS WARD.

These people delighted WARD more than all the rest. They seemed to him exquisitely funny, and there was always something in the lecture in recognition of them.

He even went the length of printing this obliging note in his programme for their benefit :

" Mr. ARTEMUS WARD will call on the citizens of London at their residences, and explain any jokes in his narrative which they may not understand."

On one occasion, in America, a lady and her two daughters rose suddenly in the middle of one of his lectures and flounced out of the room, with the indignant remark that " It was quite scandalous. to see a number of people laughing at a poor half-witted young man who evidently did not know what he was talking about ! "

When ARTEMUS arrived here in 1866 he was a dying man.

I can see him now, as he came on the narrow platform in front of his inferior panorama, and stole a glance at the densely packed room and then at his panorama.

His tall, gaunt, though slender figure; his curly light hair and large aquiline nose, which always reminded me of a macaw; his thin face flushed with consumption; his little cough, which seemed to shake him to pieces, and which he said was " wearing him out," at which we all laughed irresistibly, and then felt ashamed of ourselves, as well we might; but he himself seemed to enjoy his cough. It was all part of that odd, topsy-turvy mind in which everything appeared most natural upside down !

On first entering he would seem profoundly unconscious that anything was expected of him, but after looking at the audience, then at his own clothes, and then apologetically at his panorama, he began to explain its merits.

The fact was that ARTEMUS intended having the finest scenes that could be painted, but he gave that up on account of the expense, and then determined to get the worst as the next best thing for his purpose.

When anything very bad came up he would pause and gaze admiringly at the canvas, and then look round a little reproachfully at the company.

"'This picture," he would say, " is a great work of art ; it is an oil-painting done in petroleum. It is by the Old Masters. It was the last thing they did before dying. They did this, and then they expired. I wish you were nearer to it so you could see it better. I wish I could take it to your residences and let you see it by daylight. Some of the greatest artists in London come here every morning before daylight with lanterns to look at it. They say they never saw anything like it before, and they hope they never shall again ! "

Certain curious brown splotches appearing in the foreground, Artemus pointed gravely to them, and said—

"'These are intended for horses ; I know they are, because the artist told me so. After two years, he came to me one morning and said, 'Mr. WARD, I cannot conceal it from you any longer ; they are horses.'"

The difficulties with the moon were endless. It would rise abruptly, a great noise of cranks and wheels being heard behind the scenes. WARD would watch its progress with anxiety and ill-disguised alarm ; he would then go out and attend to it himself. Renewed disturbance with the machinery ; the moon would presently fall askew, then tumble out of the heavens altogether ; when suddenly with a vigorous spurt she would go up like a cannon-shot and stick at the top, when ARTEMUS would reappear, exhausted with his exertions, and complain that he was in want of a good "moonist," his young man having left him.

The piano playing, he added, was done by a first-rate artist, who had "once lived in the same street with Thalberg."

Nothing could be more impromptu, and therefore riveting, than his manner throughout from the moment he entered; he seemed to be doing everything for the first time and without the least preparation, and indeed he was most unlike such mechanical artists as ALBERT SMITH, who used to say he could go through his "Mont Blanc" half asleep.

ARTEMUS was always, in reality, at high pressure.

He was never twice the same; he poured out new jokes with prodigal invention, and every gesture was original and arose out of the immediate occasion.

His finger was ever on the pulse of the people; they were always absolutely in his power, whilst he flattered them by appearing to be entirely in theirs.

He would conciliate them, inspire pity, claim indulgence, throw himself upon their generosity, pretend to exert himself, to labour under a depressing sense of failure, even make capital out of his poor cough; and then he was so deeply wounded, if some very mild joke failed to elicit applause that he would stop and look reproachfully at the people until they shook with a new sense of the absurd situation.

At other times, when interrupted by laughter, he would look round with surprise, and say—

"I did not expect you to laugh at that. I can throw off numbers of those little things, but I assure you I can do better than that."

When he opened his lecture on the Mormons at the Egyptian Hall, he said, quite apologetically—

"I don't expect to do much here, but I have thought if I could make money enough to buy me a passage to New Zealand, I should feel that I had not lived in vain. I don't want to live in vain. I'd rather live at Brighton or Margate, or here."

The heat was most oppressive and the hall very crowded the day I was there, and looking up to the roof, he continued—

"But I wish, when the Egyptians built this hall (a burst of laughter), they had not forgotten the ventilation."

Apropos of nothing at all a little further on, he observed—

"I really don't care for money; I only travel round to show my clothes."

This was a favourite joke of his. He would look with a piteous expression of discomfort and almost misery at his black trousers and swallow-tail coat, a costume in which he said he was always most wretched.

"These clothes I have on," he continued, "were a great success in America." And then quite irrelevantly and rather hastily, "How often do large fortunes ruin young men! I should like to be ruined, but I can get on very well as I am!"

So the lecture dribbled on with little fragments of impertinent biography, mere pegs for slender witticisms like this :

"When quite a child I used to draw on wood. I drew a small cart-load of raw material over a wooden bridge, the people of the village noticed me, I drew their attention, they said I had a future before me ; up to that time I had an idea it was behind me."

Or this :

"I became a man. I have always been mixed up with art. I have an uncle who takes photographs, and I have a servant who takes anything he can set his hands on."

But WARD was something besides a sparkling humorist ; he was a man of character and principle ; there was nothing of the adventurer—very little even of the speculator about him.

Even in the depths of comedy he was always on the side of justice and virtue, and not with the big battalions.

" 'I ax these questions' (about Louis Napoleon), says the showman, 'my royal duke and most noble highness and imperials, because I'm anxious to know how he stands as a man. I know he's smart. He is cunnin', he is long-headed, he is grate; but onless he is *good*, he'll come down with a crash one of these days, and the Bonypartes will be busted up again. Bet yer life.' "

These comic but prophetic words were written when the late Emperor was at the climax of his power, and about the time it was so much the fashion to call the Second Empire a perfect success.

" 'Air you a preacher ?' says the royal duke, slitely sarkastical.

" 'No, sir. But I bleeve in morality. I likewise bleeve in Meetin' Houses. Show me a place where there isn't any Meetin' Houses and where preachers is never seen, and I'll show you a place where old hats air stuffed into broken winders, where the children air dirty and ragged, where gates have no hinges, where the wimin air slipshod, and where maps of the devil's wild land air painted upon men's shirt-bosums with tobacco-jooce ! ·That's what I'll show you. Let us consider what the preachers do for us before we aboose 'em.' "

ARTEMUS WARD was a worthy and lovable man; he was sound, blameless, shrewd, sensitive, and affectionate.

His devotion to his old mother was like that of a little child ; her comfort and happiness was constantly uppermost in his thoughts.

At one time he wanted to get her to England—alas, it would only have been to weep over his grave ! At another, he thought of going home to live with her after making his fortune. His fame he valued quite as much for the pleasure it gave the old lady as for the cash it brought him in.

He was the natural foe of bigotry, Pecksniffianism, and immorality of every kind. There are many hard hits at hypocrites, formalists, shams, and religious scoundrels ; but throughout the whole of his works you will not find one sneer at virtue or religion, and in spite of a few broad jokes not quite in European taste, there is not one really loose or unguarded thought.

The *Times* said of his lecture on the Mormons, " It is utterly free from offence, though the opportunities of offence are obviously numerous. Not only are his jokes irresistible, but his shrewd remarks prove him to be a man of reflection as well as a consummate humorist."

" I never stain my pages," writes ARTEMUS, " with even mild profanity. In the first place it is wicked, and in the second it is not funny."

Hingston, his faithful agent, and for long his inseparable companion, who had so many opportunities of watching him under such varied and often trying circumstances, remarks, " No man had more real reverence in his nature than ARTEMUS WARD."

CHARLES FARRAR BROWNE (*alias* ARTEMUS WARD) was born at Waterford, United States, in 1836.

He began life as a type-setter, then took to newspaper reporting, and soon (like Dickens) made a mark with jokes, which went the round of the papers. The circus presently caught up the new vein of wit.

ARTEMUS was always fond of the circus, but he did not care to sit and applaud his own jokes; he thought he might contrive to get the applause and the cash himself.

A lecture, to be constructed on peculiar principles, flashed across his mind.

Was not the public worn out with dull lectures?

Had not the time of protest arrived ?

What very excellent fooling it would be to expose the dull impostors who passed up and down the land, boring mechanics' institutes and lyceums with their pretentious twaddle, and bringing art and science into disrepute !

ARTEMUS WARD felt that the man and the hour had arrived.

L

He would bring about a mighty reaction in the public taste ; under these circumstances he conceived the appalling notion of constructing a lecture which should contain the smallest possible amount of information with the greatest quantity of fun.

It was to consist mainly of a series of incoherent and irrelevant observations, strung like a row of mixed beads upon the golden thread of his wit.

WARD started in California with an announcement that he would lecture on "The Babes in the Wood." He said he preferred this title to that of "My Seven Grandmothers."

Why, nobody knows, for there was, of course, to be as little in the lecture about *babes,* in or out of the wood, as about seven or any other number of grandmothers.

"The Babes in the Wood" was never written down ; but a few sentences only have survived of a performance which was destined to revolutionize the comic lecturing of the age.

The "Babes" seem only to have been alluded to twice— first at the beginning, when the lecturer gravely announced "The Babes" as his subject; and then, after a rambling string of irrelevant witticisms, which lasted from an hour to an hour and a half, he concluded with—

"I now come to my subject—'The Babes in the Wood.'" [Then taking out his watch, his countenance would suddenly change—surprise, followed by great perplexity! At last, recovering his former composure, and facing the difficulty as best he could, he continued :] "But I find I have exceeded my time, and will therefore merely remark, that so far as I know, they were very good babes ; they were. as good as ordinary babes." [Then, almost breaking down, and much more nervously.] "I really have not time to go into their history ; you will find it all in the story-books." [Then, getting quite dreamy,] "They died in the woods, listening to the woodpecker tapping the hollow beech tree." [With some suppressed emotion,] "It was a sad fate for them, and I pity them ; so I hope do you. Good night!"

The success of this lecture throughout California was instantaneous and decisive.

The reporters complained that they could not write for laughing, and split their pencils desperately in attempts to take down the jokes.

Every hall and theatre was crowded to hear about the " Babes," and the " Lyceum " lecturer of the period,

" What crammed hisself full of high soundin' phrases, and got trusted for a soot of black clothes,"

had nothing to do but to go home and destroy himself.

Fragments of a similar piece, spoken by ARTEMUS WARD, have survived.

It is entitled "Sixty Minutes in Africa."

" I have invited you," began the lecturer, " to listen to a discourse on Africa. Africa is my subject. It is a very large subject. It has the Atlantic Ocean on its left side, Indian Ocean on its right, and more water than you could measure at its smaller end. Africa produces blacks, ivory blacks ; they get ivory. It also produces deserts, that is the reason it is so much deserted by travellers. Africa is famed for its roses. It has the red rose, the white rose, and neg-rose, *apropos* of negroes, let me tell you a little story."

That was the signal for a digression of about an hour, during which time no further mention of Africa occurred ; when he wound up with—

" Africa, ladies and gentlemen, is my subject ; you wish me to tell you something about Africa. Africa is on the map—it is on all the maps of Africa I ever saw. You may buy a good map for a dollar, and if you study it well you will know more about Africa than I do. It is a comprehensive subject, too vast for me to enter upon to-night. If you go home and go to bed, it will be better for you than to go with me to Africa."

ARTEMUS was an insatiable rover. At one time, being laid up, he read LAYARD'S " Nineveh."

The Bulls excited his fancy ; the Arabs and the wildness of the scenes, the ignorance, stupidity, and rascality of the natives, the intelligence and enthusiasm of the explorer, the marvellous unlooked-for results—all this suited him.

He must go to Nineveh and have a look, and come back and speak a piece.

Alas! cut short at the early age of thirty, how many "pieces" had to remain unspoken, and a trip to Nineveh amongst them!

What an eye for incident that man had!

He was not devoid of poetic sensibility. He could linger sympathetically for a moment upon snow-capped mountains, or give himself up to the wild, free sensations inspired by the boundless prairie; but let him catch sight of a heathen Chinese with a pig-tail, and suddenly everything else vanishes, and WARD will turn the inexorable lens of his humour upon him, and seize his playful or any other characteristic with a bite worthy of Mr. RUSKIN.

Indeed, the love of detail is a feature common to both Mr. RUSKIN and ARTEMUS WARD.

The habit which tempts a RUSKIN away from a Greek column to examine some tiny lichen or climbing tendril at its base, is the same tendency poetically exercised which is seen humorously enough in ARTEMUS, when he forsakes yon cloud-capped mountain for a chinaman's pig-tail.

Passing from San Francisco to Salt Lake City, WARD becomes his own *raconteur*.

Of course he lectured by the way, and his progress was somewhat slow and roundabout, like that of the ant who, in order to cross the street, chose to go over the top of Strasburg Cathedral.

But the longer the journey the greater the gain to those who are anxious to surprise gleams of his quaint nature, or flashes of his wit, humour, and adventure.

In California his lecture theatres were more varied than convenient.

Now he stood behind a drinking-bar; once in a prison, the cells being filled with a mixed audience, and ARTEMUS standing at the end of a long passage into which they all opened; then in a billiard-room, or in the open air.

On one occasion the money being taken in a hat, the crown fell out and spilt the dollars.

WARD said he never could be quite sure how many dollars were taken that night, no one seemed to know.

All who knew WARD knew there was much truth in his saying, " I really don't care for money." He was the most genial, generous, free-handed of men; and, like other kindly souls, his good-nature was often imposed upon by unprincipled and heartless adventurers, who ate his dinners, laughed at his jokes, and spent his money.

Had it not been for Hingston, his faithful agent, he would have fared far worse, for WARD was not a man of business.

If his anecdotes by the way are not all strictly authentic, they are far too good to be lost.

He tells us how he visited most of the mountain towns and found theatres occasionally, to which he invariably repaired. One was a Chinese theatre. When he offered his money to the Chinaman at the door, that official observed—

" Ki hi hi ki shoolah ! "

" I tell him," says WARD, " that on the whole I think he is right."

On entering one, he finds the play is going to last six weeks; he leaves early.

It is in this rough mountainous region that some of WARD'S best jokes were manufactured. To this period belongs the famous man who owed him two hundred dollars and never paid him.

" A gentleman, a friend of mine, came to me one day with tears in his eyes ; I said, ' Why these weeps ? ' He said he had a mortgage on his farm, and wanted to borrow two hundred dollars. I lent him the money, and he went away. Some time after, he returned with more tears. He said he must leave me for ever ; I ventured to remind him of the two hundred dollars. He was much cut up ; I thought I would not be hard upon him, so I told him I would throw off one hundred dollars. He brightened up, wrung my hand with emotion. ' Mr. WARD,' he exclaimed, ' generous man ! I won't allow you to outdo me in liberality, I'll throw off the other hundred.' "

But the Salt Lake had to be reached, and a wild and to some extent perilous journey it was.

Down the slopes of precipitous mountains, in frightful darkness and snow, cheered by the driver, who relates the catastrophes of past journeys on similar occasions; then sledging the flats with Hingston in midwinter, amongst the wild miners, amongst the wilder wolves and red Indians.

On one occasion they were actually attacked by a horde of famished wolves, and, having fired all their powder and ball away, they had to come to unpleasantly close quarters and beat the beasts off with the butt end of their horse-pistols.

Soon after that, they had to leave their sledge and wade four miles knee-deep through the snow, until they regained the beaten track.

On another occasion ARTEMUS was stopped by the Indians, not far from Salt Lake City, and only released through the influence of BRIGHAM YOUNG.

The humorous account of his captivity is too long to quote and too good to shorten, but the following anecdote of his robbery by the Indians is equally characteristic, and more compendious.

Here he is surprised on the open plains.

" The chief of the red men said, ' Brothers ! the paleface is welcome. Brothers ! the sun is sinking in the west and Wanna-bucky She will soon cease speaking. Brothers ! the poor red man belongs to a race which is fast becoming extink ! '

"He then whooped in a shrill manner, stole all our blankets and whisky, and fled to the primæval forest to conceal his emotions."

In the greatest trepidation, ARTEMUS at length beheld the trim buildings of the Mormons shining in the distance, and entering the spacious thoroughfares studded with gardens, and lively with a very mixed, active, and always industrious population, sought out with Hingston a retired inn and gave himself up to his own reflections.

These were not pleasant.

He certainly meant to see Salt Lake and the Mormons, and there he was.

But in his book he had been unsparing in his sarcasms on the Mormons, BRIGHAM and all his works, and if there was one thing he felt quite certain of, it was that he was now in the absolute power of the most unscrupulous man in America, whom he happened to have grossly insulted.

Hingston advised him not to venture abroad rashly, and went out himself to see which way the wind blew.

ARTEMUS sat smoking moodily at home, expecting, as he says—

"To have his swan-like throat cut by the Danites."

At last enters a genial Mormon Elder, who assures him of the general good-will of the Mormons, but also pulls out a book ("ARTEMUS his book !") and reads to its author a passage which he admits to have somewhat hurt their feelings ; and certainly it is a little strong, as coming from a man who had never been in Salt Lake City or seen the people.

This is the passage, and it occurs in the Showman's papers.

"I girded up my lions and fled the seen ; I packed up my duds and left Salt Lake, which is a second Sodom & Gomorrer, inhabited by as thievin' and unprincipled a set of retches as ever drew breth in eny spot on the globe!' "

On hearing these awful words, of which up to that moment their writer had never felt in the least ashamed, WARD declares that his feelings may be more easily imagined than described !

He was forced to admit further that the Mormons might not be quite such " unprincipled retches " as he had described, and he parted at last with the mild and con-ciliatory Elder pleasantly enough, instead of having his swan-like throat cut.

Coals of fire were soon to be heaped on his devoted head.

Worn out with the excitement and fatigue of many days and nights of travel, he was struck down with fever.

"The thievin' and unprincipled retches " by whom he was surrounded now vied with each other to do him service, they nursed him patiently, treated him with the utmost kindness, procured him every comfort, and BRIGHAM YOUNG sent him his own doctor.

" The ladies," he says, " were most kind. I found music very soothing when I lay ill with fever in Utah ; and I was very ill,—I was fearfully wasted, and on those dismal days a Mormon lady—she was married, though not so much married as her husband, he had fifteen other wives—she used to sing a ballad commencing, ' Sweet bird, do not fly away !' I told her I would not. She played the accordion divinely, accordionly I praised her."

Of course ARTEMUS could not exactly eat his own words, or recant his deeply rooted opinions, of which he was quite as tenacious as some other men ; but he pays a warm tribute to the friendly courtesy of BRIGHAM, adding—

" If you ask me how pious he is, I treat it as a conundrum and give it up."

The moment at last arrives for him to face a Mormon audience and speak his piece.

They place the theatre at his disposal, and—

"I appear," he says, "before a Salt Lake of upturned faces!"

He is listened to by a crowded and kindly audience.

Whether it was the "Babes" or "Africa," we know not, but he mentions that some odd money was taken at the door.

The Mormons, it appeared, paid at the door in *specie*, and that of all kinds:

Such as five pounds of honey, a firkin of butter, a wolf's skin. One man tried to pass a little dog—a cross between a Scotch terrier and a Welsh rabbit; another a German-silver coffin plate. "Both were very properly declined by my agent."

ARTEMUS had a great longing to come to London and give his lecture at the Egyptian Hall.

That longing was destined to be gratified, but it was the last.

He thought "The Mormons" would do very well, and it did.

He knew his lungs were affected, and he knew he must die; but he did not quite know how soon.

He came here in 1867.

I heard him once only, about a few weeks before he died.

He looked very thin and ill.

He coughed a good deal, and could only speak for about three-quarters of an hour, but was quite irresistible.

He was soon unable to continue his entertainment. "In the fight between youth and death," writes his friend Robertson, "death was to conquer."

His doctor sent him to Jersey; but the sea breezes did him no good.

He wrote, genial and sympathetic to the end, that "his loneliness weighed on him."

He tried to get back to town, but only got as far as Southampton; there many friends went down from London to see the last of him—two at a time.

Hingston never left him, and the consul of the United States was full of the kindliest attentions.

A wealthy American had offered the PRINCE OF WALES a handsome American-built yacht.

"It seems, old fellow," said poor ARTEMUS, as he made his last joke to Hingston, who sat by him—"it seems the fashion for every one to present the PRINCE OF WALES with something. I think I shall leave him my panorama."

His cheerfulness seldom left him, except when he thought of his old mother, and then he would grow terribly sad.

But the end was at hand.

"CHARLES BROWNE," writes his friend Robertson, in modest but feeling terms, "died beloved and regretted by all who knew him, and when he drew his last breath there passed away the spirit of a true gentleman."

One of the many charms and surprises of WARD was his double character.

Between the rough Showman of his book and the refined-looking, intellectual master of wit, without a touch of personal vulgarity, the chasm seemed immense, and yet on his appearance it was instantly bridged.

The vehicle which he affected in his writings was happily chosen.

There is more in that native Showman, *nomine* ARTEMUS WARD, than meets the European eye at a glance.

He was a type—one of those originals in which America delights.

A man of the people, with little education, thrown out early upon the world ; Jack of all trades, keen, shrewd—his mind an incongruous mixture of ideas, with an eye quick to detect foibles and inconsistencies of character.

Sharp at business, full of low humour, half satirist, half buffoon, ready with equal effrontery to turn his hand to anything.

Store-keeper, nigger-driver, travelling dentist, photographer, or "going around " with a show of " wax-figgers," curiosities, wild beasts alive and stuffed.

Such a life had its advantages as well as its drawbacks.

It was the way to see many men and cities; to learn many things, some of which might as well have been let alone ; to get experience and to waste time ; to gain and to lose money, and to make jokes.

This mask yclep᷊ARTEMUS WARD was early seized by CHARLES FARRER BROWNIE.

It enabled him to utter upon all occasions, with equal confidence and loquacity, and upon every conceivable topic.

It provided him with endless situations and endless fun.

CHARLES BROWNE occasionally steps from behind the showman for a moment, but only for a momen

Instead of the grinning and coarse mask, we have then the grave, even sad look of a man noting and weighing the follies or crimes of others, and chiding, with impartial but not unkindly reproof, high and low, rich and poor.

But the moral pointed with a flash, and the mask is on again, before we have well mastered the features of the face behind it.

As for the Showman, he is as fine and far more solid a creation than LOWELL's Birdofredum Sawin, though not up to the weight of Homer Wilbur.

His bad grammar, the dialect, and the spelling suggest

a cross between the amusing vulgarity of THACKERAY'S " Jeames " and the vernacular of the " Biglow Papers."

The spelling is perhaps more original than either. The mind often receives a double shock, as it masters first the form and then the substance of such witty conceits as—

"Beests of Pray."
"I appear b 4 a C of upturned faces."
" 2 B or not 2 B ! "
" Reven noose muttons."
Or, " the Orleans Die-nasty ! "

The inflation of the ignorant stump orator, with his " feller-citizen " and his green cotton umbrella, is never quite absent.

The Showman has vague recollections of old quotations, learned off as trite phrases, and he assumes an alarming familiarity with the names and writings of the greatest men ; CICERO he will call " old Cis ! " and of SOCRATES, or, as he calls him, " old Sock," he pensively observes—

" He has left us—he is no more,"

which is probably all he knew about " old Sock."

His incapacity—so common with uneducated people—to distinguish between small things and great, is a delightful source of incongruity and amusement ; in short, when we least expect it, the regulative power of his mind is suddenly lifted, and mental and physical phenomena are jumbled up together like buttercups and hysterics.

"I came back," he says, " with my Vartoo unimpaired, but I shall have to git a new soot of clothes."

He waxes intense, and becomes highly inflammatory and poetical without the slightest cause.

Each word lashes the next into finer frenzy, until a wild but perfectly meaningless climax is reached, and the end of the fine writer or stump orator is thus attained.

"JEFFERSON DAVIS," he exclaims, "I now leave you! Farewell, my gay Saler Boy! Good-bye, my bold buccaneer! Pirut of the deep blue sea, adoo! adoo!"

His platitudes and moral sentences are always equally delightful and absurd:

"Virtoo is its own reward!"
"Be Vartoous, and you will be happy."

He is never more winning than when exposing his own humbug, or explaining his misfortunes.

How a mob caved in the head of JUDAS ISCARIOT, one of his best wax figures.

How the people pulled the hay out of the fat man, and kicked him from the show; and then discovering that the latest murderer, another wax figure, was in fact GENERAL WASHINGTON of the year before, with a new wig and moustache, smashed him to pieces; and lastly how the Showman himself narrowly escaped tarring and feathering.

Although everything is overdrawn, as in Pickwick, there is an intense reality of conception about this Showman; his various characteristics come together with such admirable ease, fitness, and effrontery, that he at last stands out as one of the most realistic and irresistibly captivating creations of modern fiction.

The Showman is hard on the woman's rights movement; but then the woman's rights in America were decidedly hard on the public.

The extravagances of Bloomerism set all decent and sensible people dead against the preposterous viragos who, in the early days, degraded a noble cause to the level of an indecent burlesque.

The Showman is pleasant enough whenever he comes face to face with an advanced advocate of woman's rights.

"On the cars," he relates, "was a he-lookin female, with a green cotton umbreller in one hand and a handful of Reform tracks in the other. She sed every woman ought to have a Spear. Them as didn't demand their Spears, didn't know what was good for them. 'What is my Spear?' she axed, addressin the peple in the cars. 'Is it to stay at home & darn stockins, & be the ser-lave of a domineerin man? Or is it my Spear to vote & speak & show myself the ekal of man? Is there a sister in these keers that has her proper Spear?' Sayin which the eccentric female whirled her umbreller round several times, & finally jabbed me in the weskit with it.

"'I hav no objecshuns to your goin into the Spear bizniss,' sez I, 'but you'll please remember I ain't a pickeril. Don't Spear me agin, if you please.' She sot down."

His treatment of the Shakers and the Spiritualists is equally sound and discerning.

The balance of his mind, *when he chooses*, is always excellent.

What can be more shrewd and genial than this?—

"'Here you air,' he says to the Shakers, 'all pend up by yerselves, talkin about the sins of a world you don't know nothin of. Meanwhile said world continners to resolve round on her own axeltree onct in every 24 hours, subjeck to the Constitution of the United States, and is a very plesant place of residence.'"

He is even scrupulously fair to opinions and people with whom he has no sort of sympathy, without showing up what he scorns as delusion or condemns as mischievous.

"'You dowtlis,' he says to the Spiritualist, 'beleve this Sperrit doctrin, while I think it is a little mixt. . . . Admittin all you say abowt the doctrin to be troo, I must say the reglar perfessional Sperrit rappers—them as makes a bizniss on it—air about the most ornery set of cusses I ever enkountered in my life.' So sayin, I put on my surtoot and went home."

The Showman's preposterous interviews with the great men of the day are not only full of local colour, but tempered with the keenest appreciation and the justest estimate of character.

Such is the sketch of ABRAHAM LINCOLN, surrounded by

place-seekers or "patrits," and labouring to steer his course straight. Enter the Showman, who begins to rage amongst the servile crew thus :

"'Go home, you miserable men, go home & till the sile ! Can't you giv Abe a minit's peace ? Go to choppin wood—go to bilin sope—stuff sassengers—black boots . . . go round as original Swiss bell ringers—becum origenal and only Campbell Minstrels . . . saw off your legs and go round givin concerts, with techin appeals to a charitable public—anything for a honest livin, but don't come here drivin Old Abe crazy by your outrajis cuttings up ! ' "

As the claimants disperse :

"'How kin I ever repay you, sir ?' exclaims the President.
" 'By givin the whole country a good, sound administration. By poerin ile upon the troubled waturs, north and south. By pursooin a patriotic, firm, and just course, and then if any State wants to secede, let 'em secesh ?
"'How 'bout my Cabinit, Mister Ward ?' sed Abe.
"Fill it up with Showmen, sir ! Showmen is devoid of politics. They hain't got any principles ! . . . Showmen is honest men ! ' "

The boldest and perhaps the most amusing of all these interviews is that with the Prince of Wales, who was then a very young man, travelling in the United States.

In the hands of a lesser artist, the colloquy must have run to the very verge of insolence. In the hands of Artemus, it merely leaves a just and graphic impression of the Prince of Wales's unaffected and manly simplicity, which so struck the Americans and has remained one of his most pleasing characteristics.

" I axed him," says the showman, "how he liked bein Prince, as fur as he'd got.
" 'To speak plain, Mr. Ward,' he sed, 'I don't much like it. I'm sick of all this bowin & scrapin & crawlin & hurrain over a boy like me. I would rather go thro' the country quietly & enjoy myself in my own way, with the other boys, & not be made a show of. . . . You know, Mr. Ward, I can't help bein a Prince, & I must do all I kin to fit myself fur the persishun I must sum time ockepy.

" I rose up & said, ' Albert Edard, I must go, but previs to doin so
I will obsarve that you soot me. . . . When you git to be king, try & be
as good a man as yure muther was ! Be just ! be Ginerous ! ' "

Before parting with ARTEMUS, I would fain try to fix the
shifting kaleidoscopic colours as they melt and change, to
analyze what is no sooner present than it is past, to set down
the characteristics of a mind the qualities of which have
surely never been seen in such singular and fascinating
combination before, which we are never likely to see in the
smallest degree reproduced, and which has now for some
twenty years defied a host of plagiarists and imitators as
successfully as the music of Chopin or the brush of Turner.

First, I note his spontaneity.   He was quite as good at
home as abroad—in private as in public.

This was his charm.

He never knew how many odd things he was going to
say, and often forgot them afterwards.

In his entertainments he was constantly personal, yet
without ever giving offence.

In public he had the quickest tact, the kindliest humour,
and the gentlest delicacy of any man I ever saw.

His mind resembled the retina of the eye, in which everything appears naturally upside down.

Other people, like DICKENS or JOHN PARRY, went out
of their way to reverse ideas ; to WARD the reverse order
seemed always the natural one ; from his point of view the
whole world stood on its head, men thought backwards, and
words invariably meant their contraries.

The shock of this incessant and easy inversion is irresistible ; as when describing a temperance hotel, where, he
says, they sold the very worst liquors he ever tasted.   He
goes on to say—

" I don't drink now ; I've given all that up.   I used to drink once ;
but when I did, I never allowed business to interfere with it."

Or when he remarks that he had always been of opinion that an occasional joke improved a comic paper. At first we suppose it to be a kind of *lapsus linguæ*. Not at all; it is merely common sense backwards—a ludicrous and usually satirical reversal of ordinary ideas.

Closely akin to this, I note a steady displacement of atmosphere; as when his organ-grinder dies, he says he never felt so *ashamed* in his life.

Shame is the wrong emotion; but it is slipped in mechanically, like a drop-scene that has got out of its right place, and provides a churchyard instead of the altar-rail for a marriage ceremony.

WARD'S subtle trifling with words, as well as atmospheres, is reduced almost to a fine art, and results in quite a new and peculiar coinage.

"'Let us glide,' I said, 'in the mazy dance,' and we glode."
"Let 'm secesch !" "He's caught a tormatter."

Which is quite in Mrs. Gamp's style, with her "Not all the tortoises of the imposition"—for "tortures of the inquisition."

But in America the Malaprop seedling comes up with an odd Yankee twist, and the ARTEMUS variety of it is certainly unique.

Sense, grammar, terminations, spelling, all go awry—we hardly notice how.

We receive a series of mental back-handers, and keep laughing, a little too late, but better and better in time, as the new method begins to gain on us.

With one more example from his life amongst the Mormons, which, perhaps, though brief, includes a greater variety of wit and humour than any single passage I could

M

select, I must conclude my memorial glimpses of this incomparable and lamented humorist.

◡ THE SEVENTEEN YOUNG MORMON WIDOWS.

"I regret to say that efforts were made to make a Mormon of me while I was in Utah.

"It was leap year when I was there, and seventeen young widows —the wives of a deceased Mormon (he died by request)—offered me their hearts and hands. I called upon them one day, and taking their soft, white hands in mine—which made eighteen hands altogether—I found them in tears. And I said, 'Why is this thus?—what is the reason of this thusness?'

"They hove a sigh—seventeen sighs of different size. They said—

"'Oh, soon thou wilt be gonested away!'

"I told them that when I got ready to leave a place I usually wentested. They said—'Doth not like us?'

"I said, 'I doth, I doth!' I also said, 'I hope your intentions are honourable, as I am a lone child, and my parents are far, far away!'

"They then said—'Wilt not marry us?'

"I said, 'Oh, no; it cannot was.'

"Again they asked me to marry them, and again I declined. When they cried—

"'Oh, cruel man! This is too much—oh, too much!'

"I told them it was on account of the muchness that I declined."

V

MARK TWAIN.

V.

MARK TWAIN.

MARK TWAIN in about ten years has achieved cosmopolitan renown.

Every English-speaking market is flooded with his "Innocents" of all sorts.

About the only book I could get at Rome—outside the magic Tauchnitz circle—was "The Jumping Frog."

"Roughing it" has consoled me in some of the worst inns on the "Continong;" and whenever, like those celebrated travellers afoot, I have steadily declined to walk, and got into the nearest train, cab, carriage, boat, or railway car sooner than wear out my boots—whenever, I say, I have indulged in these easy "promenades" *en voiture*, I have been forcibly reminded of the "New Pilgrims' Progress" and the "Tramp Abroad."

Many people regard TWAIN merely as an extravagant wag with a long bow.

It is the fate of all wags. Yet a man may be more than a wag. It matters not. The direct impact power of a joke is so much quicker than that of any other known projectile, that it is sure to hit the public sooner than any other qualities in a man, however superior and forcible.

OLIVER WENDELL HOLMES never counselled more wisely

than when he said, "Make a reputation first by your more solid acquirements. You can't expect to do anything great with Macbeth, if you first come on flourishing Paul Pry's umbrella !"

Now, MARK TWAIN came on first with his "Jumping Frog," his horse "Jericho," and the bucking "Mexican Plugs."

Had he done no more, he would have deserved well of the public ; but he has done more, and in all he has done he is oddly sound and quaintly thorough besides.

I believe this is not the general view.

He is supposed to lie like truth ; but in my opinion he as often speaks truth like lies, and utters many verities in jest —ay, and in earnest too.

When serious he is, I believe, generally reliable. You can usually tell when he has got hold of the long bow, and when he is shooting fair ; and I must say, that whenever I have taken the trouble to verify his statements of fact and descriptions of scenery, I have found them minutely accurate and photographically true.

If I want to know about the shoals of that big American stream called the Mississippi, and the look of its banks, and the set of its craft, and the ways of its voyagers, I would read MARK TWAIN's "Mississippi Pilot."

DEAN STANLEY is graphic and elaborate enough on Palestine, and ERNEST RENAN touches its Past and Present like a poet and a philosopher ; but any one who wants to understand without going there exactly how it looks now, had better read the "Innocents Abroad."

The wild mining life of Nevada and California may be coloured, but it is coloured entirely in keeping with reality.

There is no difference, except in wit and graphic force, between MARK TWAIN's sketches of the swashbucklers

and bullies like "Slade" and "Arksansas" and the newspaper police reports and cuttings of the period.

The truth about Switzerland is not far to seek.

There, at least, TWAIN knows what he is about, and he
either trifles outrageously or not at all.

Nothing brief about the glaciers has ever been better put
together than his awful narrative of the men who fell into
crevices, and were yielded up by the slow-moving mass of
ice at the end of fourteen or forty years. "Home, sweet
home! there's no place like home!" more than once seemed
to me an altogether plausible sentiment as I read these
cheerful and precipitous narratives.

MARK TWAIN'S strong points are his facile but minute
observation, his power of description, a certain justness and
right proportion, and withal a great firmness of touch and
peculiar—I had almost said personal—vein of humour.

By right proportion I mean putting things substantially
in their right light.

I might almost say that TWAIN never makes a mistake
here.

At times he no doubt indulges openly in a certain
rollicking exaggeration and fun, but when he *estimates*, he is
always just—just to the wild miner, but no unscrupulous
panegyrist or obsequious idolater of him, like BRET HARTE;
just to the eccentricities of tourists, whether English,
French, German, or American; and always just to religion
—never, I believe, wantonly irreverent, though occasionally
a little free with subjects too sacred in the eyes of many.to
be so lightly touched.

'Tis, after all, a fault of taste rather than of morals.

The value of religion itself is not more tenderly, than is
the sham and cant of hypocrisy severely handled.

As a Humorist, of course, TWAIN deals with the various kinds of mental shock quite inseparable from all wit and humour.

The shock of exaggeration, as in the "Jumping Frog," a conceit which to me is the least witty of all his well-known skits; for what, I should like to know, is the fun of saying that a frog who has been caused to swallow a quantity of shot cannot jump so high as he did before?

I should have said, after such a digestive exercise he could not jump at all!

The shock of the impossible, the incongruous, and a general inversion of ideas is common of course to TWAIN and every other humorist; but he seldom flashes like ARTEMUS. He *distils* his fun drop by drop through a whole page, instead of condensing it into a sentence. With every touch the atmosphere is intensified, and the picture slowly comes together until the page, or even the chapter, stands out a perfect pyramid of fun.

This is his gift—the long-drawn-out, elaborately spun witticism; the carefully finished, photographically minute picture.

That he *never* flashes I do not say, but his swiftest sallies —done in chalk, with a few strokes—are pictorial; the image is scratched firmly, unmistakably, as when he describes the passage through the Alps and down into Italy, he says, all the way through Mount Cenis and right on—

"The train is profusely decorated with tunnels."

Or when describing the effect of his own withering sarcasm upon his agent Harris, he remarks—

"When the musing spider steps on to the red-hot shovel, he first exhibits a wild surprise, then he shrivels."

MARK TWAIN'S secret is a tolerably open one.

He is always wide awake, therefore he keeps you awake.

He is full of observation, therefore he is pleasant company.

He is not too full, therefore he is not a bore.

He jokes habitually, and therefore he makes you laugh. The jokes are generally easy ones, so they do not you make think.

This is important, for the slow discovery of a joke always a wearing process

He is descriptions are so vivid that you feel, after reading them, that you know all about those places, so you need not go there.

This saves trouble.

In this way, MARK TWAIN himself ascended Mont Blanc. He found he could make the entire ascent for three francs —through the telescope.

Harris, the agent, was allowed to go with him for two more.

Harris was afraid, and did not want to go, but TWAIN "heartened him up," and said he would hold his hand all the way.

So they started, and in a very few minutes reached the top, and were able to describe the various peaks.

"The 'Yodel-horn,' and the 'Dinner-horn' and 'Scrabble-horn,' and the soaring domes of the 'Bottle-horn,' and the 'Saddle-horn,' and the 'Shovel-horn;' and in the 'west-south-west' they beheld the stately range of the Himalayas, which lay dreaming in the purple gloom."

This is very pleasant fooling, but it is not difficult, and it is evidently "*calqué*," as the French say, upon the experiences of "little Billee," who, under far more trying circumstances, beheld from the topmast of H.M.S.—

"Jerusalem and Madagascar
And North and South Amerikee."

Then last, but not least, TWAIN has shown that he can *go on.*

He is not the man of one book or one idea.

Put him down anywhere, and he will create a situation and spread like that American water-plant which infests the Cam, and has stretched itself over most English rivers.

He will soon crowd most waters he can get access to.

What can be more unlike any of his previous works than "The Prince and the Pauper," TWAIN's 1881 Christmas book? There the fun lies in the fancy that EDWARD VI., in a freak just before he ascended the throne, changed clothes with a romantic beggar boy who resembled him closely. The beggar boy is found in the palace, and the courtiers cannot be persuaded that he is not the prince; only the prince, alas! changed—gone mad! Meanwhile, the prince, once in the beggar's clothes, cannot convince any one outside the palace that he is really the king in disguise. So the freak ends in a prolonged struggle on both sides, the prince trying to get back to the palace; the beggar at first trying to get out of the palace, then whimsically resigning himself, up to the moment of coronation, when the *dénouement,* of course, is managed, as intellectual readers will find set down in quaint English in this same showy picture-book.

In freshness and fertility TWAIN resembles poor ARTEMUS, and rises above BRET HARTE, though he is less intense and pathetic than the latter.

ARTEMUS, like TWAIN, rejoiced in variety. He created everywhere; you could not play him out.

In California or the great lone silver land, a new pilgrims' progress was ever before him.

Most men who can write at all can write one book if they try, but many men can do no more.

I confess I do not care much for your dog with one trick,
and the public soon get tired of him.

SAMUEL LANGHORNE CLEMENS, *alias* MARK TWAIN, was
born in Florida, 1835.

He began life as a printer.

You cannot take up any of his books without noticing
what an eye he has for a sentence in type.

His punctuation is elaborate to a fault.

I should think his use of commas and full stops would
run any office dry, let alone the hyphens.

He coined his *nom de plume* on the Mississippi. He
very soon took to the river, and, working as a pilot, he often
had occasion to hear the warning cry, " Mark Twain ! " or
" In two fathoms ! " and when he came to write for the
newspapers, he signed himself " MARK TWAIN ! "

In 1861 he went to Nevada as secretary to his brother,
who was acting as a kind of government agent in that wild,
silver-mining, dismal land.

In " Roughing it " he has given us some idea of what he
did not do, as well as of what he did and was done to, out
there.

In 1864 he visited the Hawaian Islands, and has left us
such a description of a burning crater some miles round,
and full of white and red heated crystal fire caverns and
crimson lava, that henceforth the poor creatures who have
only been up Vesuvius had better hide their diminished
heads.

In 1867 he made his *début* as a comic writer with the
" Jumping Frog " and other sketches, most of them better
than the " Frog."

In 1869 he married a rich lady, but was soon again on
the tramp, this time through the Holy Land.

He now becomes the " Innocent Abroad," and relates,

with the assistance of the guide-book, the adventures and progress of the New Pilgrims.

In 1872 he visited England and lectured, without, I believe, striking success.

I heard him once at the old Hanover Square Rooms. The audience was not large nor very enthusiastic. I believe he would have been an increasing success had he stayed longer.

We had not time to get accustomed to his peculiar way, and there was nothing to take us by storm, as in ARTEMUS WARD.

He came on and stood quite alone.

A little table, with the traditional water-bottle and tumbler, was by his side.

His appearance was not impressive, not very unlike the representation of him in the various pictures in his " Tramp Abroad."

He spoke more slowly than any other man I ever heard, and did not look at his audience quite enough.

I do not think that he felt altogether at home with us, nor we with him.

We never laughed loud or long ; no one went into those irrepressible convulsions which used to make ARTEMUS pause and look so hurt and surprised.

We sat throughout expectant and on the *qui vive*, very well interested, and gently simmering with amusement.

With the exception of one exquisite description of the old Magdalen ivy-covered collegiate buildings at Oxford University, I do not think there was one thing worth setting down in print.

I got no information out of the lecture, and hardly a joke that would wear, or a story that would bear repeating.

There was a deal about the dismal, lone silver-land, the

story of the Mexican plug that bucked, and a duel which never came off, and another duel in which no one was injured; and we sat patiently enough through it, fancying that by-and-by the introduction would be over, and the lecture would begin, when TWAIN suddenly made his bow and went off!

It was over. I looked at my watch; I was never more taken aback. I had been sitting there exactly an hour and twenty minutes!

It seemed ten minutes at the outside.

If you have ever tried to address a public meeting, you will know what this means.

It means that MARK TWAIN is a consummate public speaker.

If ever he chose to say anything, he would say it marvellously well; but in the art of saying nothing in an hour, he surpasses our most accomplished parliamentary speakers.

Perhaps you will think it time for me to come to business. A cynical friend said to me the other day—

"Do you know what makes a good lecturer?"

"Haven't an idea," said I.

"Well, the first thing is to know what to leave out."

"That's good," I replied.

"The second thing is to know what to put in."

"That's better."

"And do you know what is the last?"

I gave it up.

"To know when to leave off!" he replied.

"Best of all!" I said.

Then eyeing me uncomfortably, he added—

"And which do you think I advise most men to begin with."

" Which ? " I said anxiously.

" The last ! "

" Well," I said, " I don't call that giving a man fair encouragement ; but I shall follow up the first three points."

Travel is evidently the characteristic fount of TWAIN's inspiration. He loves to be on the move, and make notes by the way. I will label him for this occasion under his three great travelling heads :

First, phases of the Holy Land, or the " New Pilgrims' Progress," and " Innocents Abroad."

Second, phases of Nevada and California, or " Roughing it " and the " Innocents at Home."

Third, phases of European travel, or " A Tramp Abroad," chiefly in Switzerland.

In 1869 this Innocent set out to explore the Holy Land and Egypt, stopping by the way at Athens.

It was but a glimpse, but it is one of the most vivid vignettes by moonlight on record.

Forbidden to land by the authorities, four of them stole ashore at midnight, clambered stealthily over the " rocky, nettle-grown eminence," and soon woke up the dogs. Over the loose calcareous soil they hurried, towards the heights of the Acropolis, presently entangling their feet in grape vines, they paused to feed on the delicious grapes, until a dark shape arose out of the shadows and said, " Ho ! " and so they left.

They find the Acropolis locked. The garrison turns out, and is bribed, and so they enter.

Then the inevitable feeling which seizes all travellers who first stand amidst those peerless ruins, came over them.

It is an awe and admiration quite distinct from anything experienced at Rome or elsewhere.

The Greek touch is ineffable; the Greek spirit and subtlety of beauty is as alive as ever, and haunts that Athenian summit, strewn all over with the fragments of Praxiteles and Phidias.

"We walked out into the grass-grown, fragment-strewn court beyond the Parthenon. It startled us every now and then, to see a stony white face stare suddenly up at us out of the grass with its dead. The place seemed alive with ghosts. I half expected to see the Athenian heroes of twenty centuries ago glide out of the shadows, and steal into the old temple they knew so well and regarded with such boundless pride.

"The full moon was riding high in the heavens now. We sauntered carelessly and unthinkingly to the edge of the lofty battlements of the citadel, and looked down. A vision!—and such a vision! Athens by moonlight! It lay in the level plain, right under our feet—all spread abroad like a picture, and we looked upon it as we might be looking at it from a balloon. We saw no semblance of a street, but every house, every window, every clinging vine, every projection were marked as clearly as it were at noonday; and yet there was no glare, no glitter, nothing harsh or repulsive. The harshest city was flooded with the yellowest light that ever streamed from the moon, and seemed like some living creature wrapped in peaceful slumber. On its further side was a little temple, whose delicate pillars and ornate front glowed with a rich lustre that chained the eye like a spell; and nearer by, the palace of the king reared its creamy walls out of the mist of a great garden of shrubbery, that was flecked all over with a random shower of amber lights—a spray of golden sparks that lost their brightness in the glory of the moon, and glinted softly upon the sea of dark foliage like the pallid star of the milky way. Overhead the stately columns, majestic still in their ruin; underfoot, the dreaming city; in the distance, the silver sea. The picture needed nothing. It was perfect."

You see that TWAIN can pause to paint a picture when he pleases.

When he reaches Palestine, his sketches of the holy places are, to say the least, realistic, and exceedingly vivid.

"They are not," he writes, "as deliriously beautiful as the books paint them. If one be calm and resolute, he can look upon their beauty and live."

It is well to know the worst.

Neither STANLEY nor RENAN have concealed from us the real condition of that strip of coast-land, once the busy mart of the world, thronged with prosperous cities, and alive with an eager and enterprising population, now bereaved and lonely.

"Palestine sits in sackcloth and ashes. Over it broods the spell of a curse that has withered its fields and fettered its energies."

"Nazareth is forlorn; about that ford of Jordan, where the hosts of Israel entered the Promised Land with songs of rejoicing, one finds only a squalid camp of fantastic Bedouins of the desert; Jericho lies a mouldering ruin. Bethlehem and Bethany, in their poverty and their humiliation, have nothing now to remind one that they once knew the high honour of the Saviour's presence; the hallowed spot where the shepherds watched their flocks by night, and where the angels sang 'Peace on earth, good will to men,' is untenanted by any living creature. Renowned Jerusalem itself, the stateliest name in history, has lost all its ancient grandeur, and is become a pauper village. The noted Sea of Galilee, where Roman fleets once rode at anchor and the disciples of the Saviour sailed in their ships, was long ago deserted by the devotees of war and commerce, and its borders are a silent wilderness; Capernaum is a shapeless ruin; Magdala is the house of beggared Arabs; Bethsaida and Chorazin have vanished from the earth, and the 'desert places' round about them, where thousands of men once listened to the Saviour's voice, sleep in the hush of a solitude that is inhabited only by birds of prey and skulking foxes."

That is what the government of the Turk has done.

Mr. GLADSTONE was not far wrong when he spoke of clearing him, *i.e.* his government, bag and baggage, out of Europe.

The Turkish peasant is a quiet, industrious creature; but the dissolute Pashas, the governing classes at Constantinople, are utterly corrupt—these are the people to be cleared out.

Let me know the state of a country, and I will tell you whether it is governed rightly or not.

The portions of the earth over which the Turk has ruled

for centuries are blighted and blasted, the population has dwindled, the soil is sterile, reedy marsh lands have taken the place of waving corn-fields, the rivers are choked, the harbours are blocked;—yet once Palestine and Asia Minor were the gardens of the Roman empire and the granaries of the world !

On leaving a large continental hotel, where service has been well charged for in the bill, you may resent the file of patient domestics, from the head chamber-maid to the deputy boots, who eye you out, mutely saying, "Give ! give ! "

But go you " away down " east, and you will then know what blackmail means.

These French lackeys and Swiss scullions are trifles; these handmaids are poor novices compared to your true Arab.

"If you hire a man to sneeze for you," says TWAIN, pathetically, "and another chooses to help him, you have got to pay both."

And he adds, with his usual touch of keen observation—

"How it must have surprised such people to hear the way of salvation offered them without money and without price ! "

Romance and comfort do not always go together. I have often noticed that the picturesque means the ramshackle; and, much as we may abuse beaten tracks, there are advantages in the snug rooms and wholesome food of a good hotel, which, like some other good things, come to be loved only when lost.

Let us arrive, fagged out with a hot sun, at the close of a long day, with wretched beasts worn to skeletons, ourselves dusty and dirty and draggled, very hungry, very sleepy, very thirsty, and very cross—say what you will, a bath, a well-

N

cooked dinner and a clean bed have their merits; but, as you are a New Pilgrim, this is your lot :

" We had to camp in an Arab village. * We could have slept in the largest house, but there were some little drawbacks—it was populous with vermin, it was in no respect cleanly, and there was a family of goats in the only bedroom and two donkeys in the parlour."

To arise from such dreams as this, and face another and another day through the desert, to such another oasis, and so on, requires health and what the Roman emperor on his death-bed called " Equanimity."

Pleasant excitement and a deplorable beast carry the pilgrim through the fearful perils of the way, which may be summed up in the one word " Bedouin."

This eastern bug-bear may be considered as finally exploded by MARK TWAIN.

The fierce and predatory Bedouin is as much a luxury organized for the delight of travellers as the chained eagle of the Alps, the captive chamois, or the castle on the Rhine (said by some to be regularly repaired and occasionally built by Cook and Gaze).

Now for the fierce and predatory Bedouin !

The Eastern traveller is fitted out with an expensive and numerous Arab guard, and the Arabs have, of course, to provide the robbers, off whom they get their living.

"The Bedouins," we read, "that attacked the other parties of pilgrims so fiercely, were provided for the occasion by the Arab guards of those parties, and shipped from Jerusalem for temporary service as Bedouins. They met together in full view of the pilgrims after the battle, and took luncheon, divided the *bucksheesh* extorted in the season of danger, and then accompanied the cavalcade home."

Still, without the institution of the Bedouins, the pilgrims would find the desert even more blank than it is. The following is a specimen of their maintien and deportment in the face of imaginary peril :—

"I think that we all must have determined on the same line of tactics, for it did seem as if we never would get to Jericho. I had a notoriously slow horse, but somehow I could not keep him in the rear to save my neck. He was for ever showing up in the lead. In such cases I trembled a little, and got down to fix my saddle. But it was not of any use. The others all got down to fix their saddles too. I never saw such a time of saddles. It was the first time any of them got out of order for three weeks, and now they had all broken down at once."

Presently, in good sooth, there is a cry raised, "Bedouins!"

"Every man shrunk up and disappeared in his clothes like a mud-turtle. My first impulse was to dash forward and destroy the Bedouins. My second to dash to the rear to see if any more were coming that way. I acted on the latter impulse; and so did all the others. If any Bedouins had approached us then from that point of the compass, they would have paid dearly for their rashness. We all remarked that, afterwards, there would have been scenes of riot and bloodshed there that no pen could describe. I know that, because each man told what he *would* have done, individually; and such a medley of strange, unheard-of inventions of cruelty you could not conceive of."

Egypt is at last reached, and of course the pyramids are interviewed. The incomparable description of the double ascent of Cheops by the pilgrims and the native athletes is one of the TWAIN gems which should be read *in extenso*, but which in its abridged form is good enough to make the head swim and the limbs totter. The pilgrims' ascent:

"Each step being full as high as a dinner-table; there being very, very many of the steps; an Arab having hold of each of our arms and springing upward from step to step and snatching us with them, forcing us to lift our feet as high as our breasts every time, and do it rapidly, and keep it up till we were ready to faint, who shall say it is not a lively, exhilarating, lacerating, muscle-straining, bone-wrenching, and perfectly excruciating and exhausting pastime, climbing the Pyramids? I beseeched the Arabs not to twist *all* my joints asunder; I iterated, reiterated, even *swore* to them that I did not wish to beat anybody to the top; did all I could to convince them that if I got there the last of all I would feel blessed above men and grateful to them for ever.

*　　*　　*　　*　　*　　*

"Twice, for one minute, they let me rest while they extorted bucksheesh, and then continued their maniac flight up the Pyramid. They wished to beat the other party. It was nothing to them that I, a stranger, must be sacrificed upon the altar of their unholy ambition.

*   *   *   *   *   *

"On the one hand, a mighty sea of yellow sand stretched away towards the ends of the earth, solemn, silent, shorn of vegetation, its solitude uncheered by any forms of creature life ; on the other, the Eden of Egypt was spread below us—a broad green floor, cloven by the sinuous river, dotted with villages, its vast distances measured and marked by the diminishing stature of receding clusters of palms. It lay asleep in an enchanted atmosphere. There was no sound, no motion. Above the date plumes in the middle distance swelled a domed and pinnacled mass, glimmering through a tinted exquisite mist ; away toward the horizon a dozen shapely pyramids watched over ruined Memphis; and at our feet the bland, impassable Sphynx looked out upon the picture from her throne in the sands as placidly and pensively as she had looked upon its like full fifty lagging centuries ago."

The Arab's ascent :

"The traditional Arab proposed, in the traditional way, to run down Cheops, across the eighth of a mile of sand intervening between it and the tall pyramid of Cephron, ascend to Cephron's summit, and return to us on the top of Cheops—all in nine minutes by the watch, and the whole service to be rendered for a single dollar. In the first flush of irritation, I was opposed to giving aid and comfort to this infidel. But stay. The upper third of Cephron was coated in dressed marble, smooth as glass. A blessed thought entered my brain. He must infallibly break his neck. We closed the contract with despatch, and let him go. He started. We watched. He went bounding down the vast broadside, spring after spring, like an ibex. He grew small and smaller till he became a bobbing pigmy, away down toward the bottom—then disappeared. We turned and peered over the other side. Forty seconds —eighty seconds—a hundred—happiness, he is dead already ! Two minutes and a quarter. 'There he goes!' Too true—it was too true. He was very small now. Gradually, but surely, he overcame the level ground. He began to spring and climb again. Up, up, up ; at last he reached the smooth coating—now for it. But he clung to it with toes and fingers, like a fly. He crawled this way and that—away to the right, slanting upward, away to the left, still slanting upward—and stood at last, a black peg on the summit, and waved his pigmy scarf ! Then he crept downward to the raw steps again, then picked up his agile heels and flew. We lost him presently. But presently again we saw him under us, mounting with undiminished energy. Shortly he bounded into our midst with a gallant war-whoop. Time—eight minutes, forty-one seconds. He had won ! "

I feel this description saves me the trouble of going there. It is as good—nay, better, for in reading it you risk neither life nor property, and have the luxury of feeling both in jeopardy at another's expense.

Before taking a peep at Nevada and the silver and gold land, I will indulge in an "interlude" on chamber-maids. This is to show that MARK TWAIN's powers of observation are always equally active. He does not require the stimulus of the Bedouin or the Arab.

Mary Jane will do.

This episode is also moral. It is a keen satire upon that habit of mind which imputes to others feelings and motives to which they may be entire strangers, and so judges them on a false issue.

Half the quarrels and spites of life arise in this way.

You impute to people your own ill humour; you fancy their genial smile is satirical.

They ask after your health ; you suspect a sinister motive.

We have all heard of the captious man who met his friend Smith one fine day.

Smith, in bursting health and spirits, slaps Brown on the back.

" Well, Brown ! how d'ye do ; and how's your wife ? "

Brown, bilious and choleric, with a menacing grunt, " H'm !—if it comes to that, *how's yours ?* "

The indictment against chamber-maids is a pungent specimen of the transference of our own feelings to others, of a certain incapacity to see things through their eyes, of an unreasoning want of consideration for them, and of an utter inability to make allowance for people of neglected education and poor intelligence.

"Against all chamber-maids . . . I launch the curse of bachelordom !
Because :

"They always put the pillows at the opposite end of the bed from
the gas-burner, so that while you read and smoke before sleeping (as is
the ancient and honoured custom of bachelors), you have to hold your
book aloft, in an uncomfortable position, to keep the light from dazzling
your eyes. . . .

"If they cannot get the light in an inconvenient position any other
way, they move the bed.

"If you pull your trunk out six inches from the wall, so that the lid
will stay up when you open it, they always shove that trunk back again.
They do it on purpose.

"They always put your boots into inaccessible places. They chiefly
enjoy depositing them as far under the bed as the wall will permit. It
is because this compels you to get down in an undignified attitude and
make wild sweeps for them in the dark with the bootjack. . . .

"They always put the matchbox in some other place. They hunt up
a new place for it every day, and put up a bottle, or other perishable
glass thing, where the box stood before. This is to cause you to break
that glass thing, groping in the dark, and get yourself into trouble. . . .

"They always save up all the old scraps of printed rubbish you throw
on the floor, and stack them up carefully on the table, and start the fire
with your valuable manuscripts. If there is any one particular old
scrap that you are more down on than any other, and which you are
gradually wearing out your life trying to get rid of, you may take all the
pains you possibly can in that direction, but it won't be of any use,
because they will always fetch that old scrap back and put it in the
same old place again every time. It does them good.

"They keep always trying to make your bed before you get up, thus
destroying your rest and inflicting agony upon you ; but after you get
up, they don't come any more till next day."

This is rather rough on Mary Jane, but not a bit rougher
than we are apt to be upon some other people whom we
dislike or do not care to understand, or towards whom we
entertain one of those indescribable antipathies which
belong to the magnetic region of the occult sympathies.

But we must now hie to wilder regions, in which MARK
TWAIN is as much at home as BRET HARTE.

Once in the rough mining regions, adventure, imagery,

tragedy, comedy succeed each other with bewildering ease and rapidity, and—

" Information," as he remarks, " stews out of him like otto of roses out of the otter."

Here we read how the mining bubble companies are floated, by adventurers arriving in large numbers with little lumps of mineral full of gold or silver ore, and persuading their ready dupes that in some distant territory the whole soil is of that peculiar make.

Here we learn how fortunes are won and lost; the odd rules of business, and the odder morality, and the oddest immorality. Indeed, the appalling scenes of violence and murder which pass before our eyes leave us bewildered and stunned, as we read of the bully Arkansas, the famous " old Sledge," and "Slumgullion" drinkers, or the portentous Slade.

Scene—a rude bar-room. Enter Arkansas, with revolvers in his belt and bowie-knives in his boots.

This is the great mining bully, dreaded, admired, and always "suffering for a fight." He is bent on one now. The meek landlord is his victim to-day. He means to goad him into a quarrel. Arkansas had been at the inn three days, and got no one to fight. On the fourth morning Arkansas got drunk. Presently Johnson the landlord came in, just comfortably social with whiskey.

" ' I reckon the Pennsylvania 'lection——' began the inoffensive host.

" Arkansas raised his finger impressively, and Johnson stopped. Arkansas rose unsteadily, and confronted him. Said he—

" ' Wha—what do you know a—about Pennsylvania? Answer me that. Wha—what do you know 'bout Pennsylvania?'

" ' I was only goin' to say——'

" ' You was only goin' to *say*. *You* was! You was only goin' to say—*what* was you goin' to say! That's it! That's what *I* want to know. *I* want to know wha—what you (*hic*)—what you know about Pennsylvania, since you're makin' yourself so d—d free. . Answer me that !'

"'Mr. Arkansas, if you'd only let me——'

"'Who's a-hinderin' you ? Don't you insinuate nothing agin me !—don't you do it. Don't you come in here bullyin' around, and cussin', and goin' on like a lunatic—don't you do it. 'Coz *I* won't *stand* it. If fight's what you want, out with it ! I'm your man ! Out with it !'

"Said Johnson, backing into a corner, Arkansas following menacingly—

"'Why, I never said nothing, Mr. Arkansas. You don't give a man no chance. I was only goin' to say that Pennsylvania was goin' to have an election next week—that was all—that was everything I was goin' to say. I wish I may never stir if it wasn't.'

"'Well, then why d'n't you say it ? What did you come swellin' around that way for, and tryin' to raise trouble ?'

"'Why, I didn't come swellin' around, Mr. Arkansas. I just——'

"'I'm a liar, am I ! Ger—reat Cæsar's ghost——'

"With that Arkansas began to shoot, and the landlord to clamber over benches and men and every sort of obstacle in a frantic desire to escape."

These atrocious villains seem to have had their use.

They provided the only type of unscrupulous rowdy which was respected by the other rowdies.

A man as absolutely indifferent to the lives of others as to his own was a power in that wild land, and the Government occasionally placed such men in a kind of authority over certain rough districts, and they found their vocation there in shooting down and bowie-kniving all who refused to obey the rude laws which served to protect property in the lone silver land, if not life.

It is some comfort to know that the end of these unprincipled swashbucklers was invariably to be stuck in the back, shot, or hanged.

The old mail-coach,

"With six wild mules, who could with difficulty be prevented from climbing the trees," yields one or two striking episodes.   Here is one :

"And once, in the night, they attacked the stage-coach when a district judge, of Nevada territory, was the only passenger, and with their first volley of arrows (and a bullet or two) they riddled the stage curtains, wounded a horse or two, and mortally wounded the driver. The latter was full of pluck, and so was his passenger.   At the driver's call Judge Nott flung himself out, clambered to the box and seized the reins of the team, and away they plunged, through the racing mob of skeletons and under a hurtling storm of missiles.   The stricken driver had sunk down on the boot as soon as he was wounded, but had held on to the reins, and said he would manage to keep hold of them till relieved.   And after they were taken from his relaxing grasp, he lay with his head between Judge Nott's feet, and tranquilly gave directions about the road.   He said he believed he could live till the miscreants were outrun and left behind, and that if he managed that, the main-difficulty would be at an end ; and then, if the judge drove so and so (giving directions about bad places in the road, and general course), he would reach the next station without trouble.   The judge distanced the enemy, and at last rattled up to the station, and knew that the night's perils were done ; but there was no comrade-in-arms for him to rejoice with, for the soldierly driver was dead."

The Penny Post comes in for its share of dashing description, which runs us a little out of breath.

The Penny Post would go from Missouri to California, 1900 miles, in eight days.   So riders were always in the saddle, with four hundred horses on the gallop.   The speed was about ten miles an hour, and a horse would go fifty miles at a stretch.

"We had had a consuming desire, from the beginning, to see a pony-rider, but somehow or other all that passed us and all that met us managed to streak by in the night, and so we heard only a whiz and a hail, and the swift phantom of the desert was gone before we could get our heads out of the windows.   But now we were expecting one along every moment, and would see him in broad daylight.   Presently the driver exclaims—

" 'HERE HE COMES !'

"Every neck is stretched further, and every eye strained wider. Away across the endless dead level of the prairie a black speck appears

against the sky, and it is plain that it moves. Well, I should think so ?
In a second or two it becomes a horse and rider, rising and falling,
rising and falling—sweeping toward us nearer and nearer—growing
more and more distinct, more and more sharply defined—nearer and
still nearer, and the flutter of the hoofs comes faintly to the ear ;
another instant a whoop and a hurrah from all of us, a wave of the
rider's hand, but no reply, and man and horse burst past our excited
faces, and go winging away like a belated fragment of a storm ! "

Put MARK TWAIN on to mountain, lake, a storm at sea,
a prairie fire, or a volcano, and you need not pull out your
photographic apparatus.

His mind is a retentive lens.

He writes with the picture before him ; no outline or
tint escapes him.

Touch after touch works up the elaborate finish until
the whole stands out perfect, and far more indelible and
indestructible than any photograph or painting or sketch.

I now come to my second interlude. This time it is on
Animals.

TWAIN is a very Landseer in prose.

I wish I could give you his old horse—alas ! too familiar
to us all—who was so old and weak that he could do
nothing but lean up against a wall and think, or his
rabbit jackass of the prairie. But his camel I must not
omit. Here we have the old trick of attributing to animals
our own motives and feelings.

Their faces become human as we look; their acts are
full of intention, caprice, wantonness, villany, craft, passion,
malice.

The delicate irony sometimes blazes up into the broadest
and most extravagant humour, as in his description of the
camel.

But the master work is not the wit ; it is the astonishing

portrait of the very camel and all his works that remains
riveted on the mind.

"In Syria once, at the headwaters of the Jordan, a camel took
charge of my overcoat while the tents were being pitched, and examined
it with a critical eye, all over, with as much interest as if he had an idea
of getting one made like it ; and then, after he was done figuring on it
as an article of apparel, he began to contemplate it as an article of diet.
He put his foot on it, and lifted one of the sleeves out with his teeth,
and chewed and chewed at it, gradually taking it in, and all the while
opening and closing his eyes in a kind of religious ecstasy, as if he had
never tasted anything so good as an overcoat before in his life. Then
he smacked his lips once or twice, and reached after the other sleeve.
Next he tried the velvet collar, and smiled a smile of such contentment
that it was plain to see that he regarded that as the daintiest thing about
an overcoat. The tails went next, along with some percussion caps and
cough candy, and some fig-paste from Constantinople. And then my
newspaper correspondence dropped out, and he took a chance in that—
manuscript letters written for the home papers. But he was treading on
dangerous ground now. He began to come across solid wisdom in
those documents that was weighty on his stomach ; and occasionally he
would take a joke that would shake him up till it loosened his teeth ; it
was getting to be perilous times with him, but he held his grip with
good courage and hopefully, till at last he began to stumble on statements that not even a camel could swallow with impunity. He began
to gag and gasp, and his eyes to stand out, and his forelegs to spread,
and in about a quarter of a minute he fell over as stiff as a carpenter's
workbench, and died a death of indescribable agony. I went and
pulled the manuscript out of his mouth, and found that the sensitive
creature had choked to death on one of the mildest and gentlest statements of fact that I ever laid before a trusting public."

The still more wonderful description of the cayotte,
pursued by a dog, is too long to quote.

The " Tramp Abroad " is at once diffuse and racy.

Tramp it is not. Other people's feet are used ; journeys
are taken on mules, coaches, boats by deputy, or even by
imagination pure and simple.

Harris, the agent, is a good figure.

He does the dirty work—goes to see the dull or incon--

venient places, is sent to face any disagreeables or dangers, and is compelled to put himself at any moment into any awkward or humiliating position, that would otherwise discompose the serenity or impair the comfort of the chief traveller and historian.

Some ladies boast of having made twenty miles in a day. Of course TWAIN will not be outdone; but, idlest of travellers, he happened to have made none. It was necessary, however, to asseverate the reverse, so he mildly observes—

"I could not lie, so I told Harris to do it."

Most Anglo-Saxons and Americans experience an invincible difficulty in bowing, or in generally being polite in the right way, according to foreign ideas.

Indeed this is a serious question.

To catch every one's eye and nod, just enough and no more, when you sit down at a *table d'hôte ;* to do the same when you get up ; to judge whether the particular eye you aim at opposite belongs to a foreigner, who likes bowing and will return yours, or to a countryman, who hates bowing and will stare you out of countenance ;—these were problems which TWAIN solved by deputy : " Harris had to do it." Then, if the bow was returned, TWAIN did it; if not, both could stalk out, but only one had been snubbed.

By the way, I have often wondered why Thackeray never wrote a " Roundabout" on "bowing."

It is one of those dreadful social—I had almost said " evils," which concern alike every gentleman and every snob.

"To bow or not to bow" is often an absorbing, even agonizing question.

The difficulty is by no means confined to bowing abroad ; bowing at home is often quite as serious a nuisance.

To bow just in the right way to everybody, and do it right each time (suppose, for instance, you meet the same person six times a day at Brighton), requires so much presence of mind that absence of body is almost preferable.

I remember John Parry used to do it at the piano.

Up and down the Esplanade, walk the victims of each other's salutation.

The first time they meet, they stop, shake hands cordially, and chat a moment.

The next time, they exchange a warm " How d'ye do ? "

The third time, a hasty " Here we are again ! " accompanied by a feverish smile.

The fourth time, they hurry past with an excited nod.

The fifth time, they rush by with averted heads.

The sixth, they see the horrible crisis from afar, and turn tail : the situation has grown untenable, and they have driven each other from the Esplanade.

But this is only one case.

I asked Hawfinch, who goes everywhere, what he did at an " at home " when he met his hostess about a dozen times face to face in the same evening. He said promptly, " I never meet her but once ; if I chance to come upon her again, I always say, 'Ta ! ta !' after which neither of us need speak or notice each other, for I'm supposed to be gone."

A good hostess is in a better position than her guests ; she has her little phrase which she says to everybody.

I have been met three times in the same evening by a late lamented lady of fashion with the same beaming smile, and she always said, " Tea in the next room ! "

This did capitally ; it enabled you to hurry off in that direction.

Another hostess adopts the phrase, " Oh ! B—— is dying to know you ! " and gazes vaguely for B——.

This does well, for it enables *her* to hurry off in the pursuit of the mythical ▮——.

But what are you to do when you meet a friend with whom your wife has had a difference ? or when Jones, who serves you in Regent Street, takes off his hat to you at Margate, or offers to shake hands with you at the Louvre ? or when you meet a lady who is not quite sure that you remember her, or, worse still, a lady who is not quite sure that she remembers you ? and when you are doubtful, is it better to bow ? or when you have taken off your hat to the wrong person, or actually stopped to speak, what on earth are you to do then ?

If you have a bad memory for faces, or are known, like most public men, to a number of people whom you don't know, are you to bow right and left, and be thought insane ; or are you to cut half the people who expect recognition, and be thought churlish ?

I declare, I have lain awake worrying over these affecting problems after making some unusually bad mistake.   But a new side of the question turned up the other day.

It was owing to my last Tramp Abroad.

I was surprised and comforted, on crossing the Channel, to find that difficulties which I supposed to be confined to the awkward and insular Briton, or at most his American brother, had begun, perhaps through our barbaric ways, to work the once invariably polite Gaul.

No doubt, as MARK TWAIN has pointed out, one of the most agonizing incidents of foreign travel is this same practice of universal salutation—standing with one's hat off out-of-doors, when addressing a lady, or in the presence of government flunkies ; capping people you never knew because they happen to know the friend you are walking with ; bowing to the shoeblack at your hotel, to the scullion in the yard, to the chamber-maid on the stairs, to the secretary, to the shop-girl, to the indefinite female character seated at the desk in all the *cafés*, to the people at the *table d'hôte*, in the railway or omnibus, and I know not where besides !

Well, I confess I thought all this was understood abroad ; I went about saying, " How beautiful is this custom ! how much we have to learn in politeness ! "

. I did a little of it with great difficulty myself, and pretended to like it, and looked surprised and shocked when any one voted the whole business a bore !

Judge, then, of my astonishment upon reading the following note in the Paris *Figaro :*—

"Ought one to salute on entering a railway, omnibus, etc. ? This question, which we have submitted to our readers, has been answered differently by many correspondents. Out of twenty, eight are affirmative, twelve are negative ; we select the following replies. *Affirmative :*—

" 'When you get into a train, you enter a private or a public place, whichever you may choose to consider it. In raising your hand to your hat, you simply act in a polite manner to strangers who will do the like to you when they alight ; 'tis a simple rule of good company.'

"Here is the *Negative :*

" 'Never whilst I live ! I have paid for my place, I take it, and occupy it like the rest : they are prepared to growl at me the instant I get in, it is needless to salute them.'

"Here is another *Negative :*

" 'No ; no more need to bow in a railway than at a *café* or restaurant : you might as well bow on entering a circus ! Notice the people who bow ; they either look nervously timid, silly, or like people afraid of the police.' "

But the most remarkable sentence is this closing opinion of the editor of the *Figaro : " This last negative opinion is on the whole our own !* " Now, upon this truly awful and complex subject of continental bowing, I almost hesitate to pronounce an opinion, but one of two things is clear.

Either bowing is essential to politeness, or it is not ; if it is, the influence of the rude Briton is rapidly corrupting the polite Frenchman, who evidently won't go on bowing without a return, in which case the Briton is an importer of bad manners; or if all this bowing is not essential to politeness, why then the Briton is a public and courageous benefactor, a model of good sense, and the Frenchman ought to be thankful for being corrected.

I should like to believe this, but I have some qualms.

As naturally practised abroad, a certain almost universal grace of manner, of which this bowing is a part, seems to me to add sweetness and dignity to life.

I don't think it can be imported into England, but I confess I should be as sorry to see the Frenchman or Italian give up his bow in imitation of the Englishman (as the editor of the French *Figaro* seems to propose), as I should be annoyed to see the English shopkeeper adopting the foreign practice of haggling over the price of his goods.

Alas! how truly has some one said, "When nations meet, they exchange their vices, not their virtues!"

Personally, as to bowing at home, I intend to err steadily on the wrong side; but when I am in France and Italy, I intend to do as much like the foreigner as I can, short of wearing out my hat or wagging off my head! We have not, unfortunately, all got Harris to do it for us.

Harris, indeed, must have been in every way a model courier and *compagnon de voyage.* He is not only invited to bow promiscuously and vicariously, but he is set on to talk to doubtful people, to entertain bores, to risk remarks in foreign tongues, and generally to occupy embarrassing situations.

But even Harris draws the line at suicide, to which he is at one time politely incited by his unscrupulous associate.

On one of the lofty summits of the Alps, it occurred to the daring and enterprising TWAIN that, as all were armed with umbrellas, and the descent was likely to be tedious, the umbrella might be used as a parachute.

One of the party would, of course, go over the precipice first, just to see how the thing acted; and, the idea being novel and brilliant, TWAIN, with some emotion, had the generosity to sacrifice himself (although it was his own conception), and offer Harris the "*pas.*" Harris declined to take it.

The honour of first descending by parachute is then offered to the guide, who declines, and *seriatim* to all the company, and the idea, strange to say, has at last to be abandoned.

This proves the enterprise and generosity of TWAIN, and the pusillanimity of his companions, Harris amongst them.

The object of this and many other like narratives in "The Tramp" is to show the immense superiority of the writer to every one else; and, let me add, this appears to be the main end of a good many autobiographies, which I need not further specify.

The student of "The Tramp" will not fail to be deeply affected by the great duel between M. GAMBETTA and M. FOURTOU, in which no one is injured except, by his own account, TWAIN, who, with his usual candour and veracity, admits that he was M. GAMBETTA'S second, and that when M. FOURTOU fired, although no shot ever touched the great French statesman, his portly form sank back upon his less stalwart second and doubled him up, putting him to serious inconvenience, and breaking many of his bones.

The German eating, the German love-making, the German student-fighting, the German language, and the German sausage, all lend themselves in turn to something like literary vivisection.

TWAIN is not the first, nor will he be the last, who has felt bitter about the German cases and genders. The *der,*

o

das, den, and *dem* are very properly marshalled, condemned, and dismissed with the contempt they deserve.

"Mei*ne* gu*ten* Freun*de,* Mei*nes* gu*ten* Freun*de,* Mei*nen* gu*ten* Freund*en,* and *den* and *dem* until one feels one might better go without friends in Germany than take all this trouble about them. 'What a bother,' he cries, 'it is to decline a good male !' But that is nothing to the trouble we are landed in by the female ! Every man has a gender, and there is no sense or system in the distribution. In German a young lady has no sex, while a turnip has. Thus you say—

"'Wilhelm, where is the turnip ?'

"'She has gone to the kitchen.'

"Or—

"'Where is the accomplished young lady?'

"'It has gone to the opera !'"

The beautiful plan of putting jumbled compounds together, is happily illustrated in the following bit of neat penny a lining extracted from a Mannheim paper :—

" In the daybeforeyesterdayshortlyafter eleveno'clock night, the inthistownstandingtavern called 'The Waggoner' was downburnt. When the fire to the onthedownburninghouseresting storks' nest reached, flew the parent storks away. But when the bytheraging fire surrounded nest *itself* caught fire, straightway plunged the quick-returning mother-stork into the flames and died, her wings over her young ones outspread."

I wish I could pause to give that entire and exhaustive instruction in the German language, to be found in the Appendix, from which I have extracted these gems ; but, as ARTEMUS WARD used to say, I should soon "find that I had exceeded my time."

In this Tramp there are flashes which often remind us of poor ARTEMUS. They are not frequent, but the influence of the earlier master is as manifest as in a school picture.

Such is the saying about Baden :—

"I left my rheumatism there ; Baden-Baden is welcome to it. It was little, but it was all I had to give. I should have liked to leave something more catching, but it was not in my power."

But the sly bit about the cuckoo clock, which is finely explosive towards the close, with the most caustic dig at the critics, deserves unabridged quotation. It is TWAIN, the whole Twain, and nothing but the Twain.

"For years my pet aversion had been the cuckoo clock; now here I was, at last, right in the creature's home; so wherever I went, that distressing '*hoo*-hoo! *hoo*-hoo! *hoo*-hoo!' was always in my ears. For a nervous man this was a fine state of things. Some sounds are hatefuller than others, but no sound is quite so inane, and silly, and aggravating as the '*hoo*-hoo' of a cuckoo clock, I think. I bought one, and am carrying it home to a certain person's; for I have always said that if the opportunity ever happened, I would do that man an ill-turn. What I meant was that I would break one of his legs, or something of that sort; but in Lucerne I instantly saw that I could impair his mind. That would be more lasting, and more satisfactory every way. So I bought the cuckoo clock; and if I ever get home with it, he is 'my meat,' as they say in the mines. I thought of another candidate—a book reviewer, whom I could name if I wanted to—but after thinking it over, I didn't buy him a clock. I couldn't injure his mind."

I consider that TWAIN is, as a rule, exceedingly fair, even in his most sportive criticisms; but I do not always agree with his opinions, even when they are evidently half serious.

I do not admit that—

"Listening to WAGNER'S music is like having toothache in the pit of the stomach."

I do not admit that there is no music in "Lohengrin," except the "Wedding Chorus," which is, of course, a pretty passable snatch of melody fit for the pert pages who sing it, but his amusing satire at the expense of the salaried and superannuated tenors is quite just and equally harmless.

"The lady was full of the praises of the head-tenor, who had performed in a Wagner opera the night before, and went on to enlarge upon his old and prodigious fame, and how many honours had been lavished upon him by the princely houses of Germany. Here was another surprise. I had attended that very opera, in the person of my agent, and had made close and accurate observations. So I said—

" ' Why, madam, *my* experience warrants me in stating that that tenor's voice is not a voice at all, but only a shriek—the shriek of a hyena.'

" ' That is very true,' she said ; ' he cannot sing now. It is already many years that he has lost his voice, but in other times he sang—yes, divinely ! So whenever he comes now, you shall see—yes, that the theatre will not hold the people. *Jawohl bei Gott!* his voice is *wunderschön* in that past time.'

" The English-speaking German gentleman who went with me to the opera there, was brimming with enthusiasm over that tenor. He said—

" ' *Ach Gott!* a great man ! You shall see him. He is so celebrate in all Germany ; and he has a pension, yes, from the government. He is not obliged to sing now, only twice every year ; but if he not sing twice each year they take him his pension away.'

" Very well, we went. When the renowned old tenor appeared I got a nudge and an excited whisper—

" ' Now you see him ! '

" But the ' celebrate ' was an astonishing disappointment to me. If he had been behind a screen, I should have supposed they were performing a surgical operation on him. I looked at my friend. To my great surprise he seemed intoxicated with pleasure ; his eyes were dancing with eager delight. When the curtain at last fell, he burst into the stormiest applause, and kept it up until the afflictive tenor had come three times before the curtain to make his bow. While the glowing enthusiast was swabbing the perspiration from his face, I said—

" ' I don't mean the least harm, but really, now, do you think he can sing ? '

" ' Him ! *No! Gott in Himmel, aber,* how he has been able to sing twenty-five years ago ! ' Then pensively. ' *Ach,* no, *now* he not sing any more ; he only cry. When he think he sing now, he not sing at all, no ; he only make like a cat which is unwell.' "

VI.
BRET HARTE.

VI.

BRET HARTE.

I WILL say a few words only about BRET HARTE. Rather than not "do him justice," as the saying is, it might have been better to leave him out of my list altogether; but perhaps even this brief tribute to a life-work yet in progress, may not be thought out of place at the close of this volume.

BRET HARTE is a man of few jokes but much humour.

The little he has to say is new, and the world does not seem to mind how often he says it.

The shorter he is the racier. When long, he invariably runs to seed.

The sphere of his attempt is wide, the range of his power narrow.

The strangeness of the new *mise en scène* took the Old World by storm; it not unnaturally asked for more. It has got draught after draught, but never a draught so strong as the "Luck of Roaring Camp;" never one so sweet as "Santa Claus," so witching as "Miggles," so naïve as "Mliss," so weird and genuine as "The Outcasts of Poker's Flat."

Poem after poem has dropt from the same facile pen;

patriotic songs on the right side, seizing the pathetic and poetic aspects of the great struggle between North and South.

Songs with a ring of LOWELL, but less firm and less strong and masterful; with a ring of POE, but without POE'S demon; with a ring of Longfellow, without his simple grace and tenderness.

But amongst them all, to my mind there is never another song like the "Plain Language of Truthful James" about the heathen Chinee.

He suddenly strikes "ile and finds his element."

A feature not the loveliest is caught as by the rays of inexorable sunlight and fixed for ever.

To the average European it is a statement, delicious, new, and perfectly convincing.

Few of us in England know much about the Chinaman.

He is one of the side-lights of modern life.

His characteristics are in danger of being overlooked.

There is good in him, which in other papers like " Wan Lee " has been duly recognized—patience, fidelity, and singular skill, and an almost stoical resignation; but here, at any rate, is some evil of him incomparably told :

" PLAIN LANGUAGE FROM TRUTHFUL JAMES.

" Which I wish to remark—
    And my language is plain—
That for ways that are dark,
    And for tricks that are vain,
The Heathen Chinee is peculiar,
    Which the same I would rise to explain.

" Ah-Sin was his name ;
    And I shall not deny
In regard to the same
    What that name might imply:
But his smile it was pensive and childlike,
    As I frequent remark'd to Bill Nye.

" It was August the third ;
   And quite soft was the skies :
Which it might be inferr'd
   That Ah-Sin was likewise ;
Yet he play'd it that day upon William
   And me in a way I despise.

"Which we had a small game,
   And Ah-Sin took a hand :
It was euchre. The same
   He did not understand ;
But he smiled as he sat by the table,
   With the smile that was childlike and bland.

" Yet the cards they were stock'd
   In a way that I grieve ;
And my feelings were shock'd
   At the state of Nye's sleeve,—
Which was stuff'd full of aces and bowers,
   And the same with intent to deceive.

" But the hands that were played
   By that Heathen Chinee,
And the points that he made,
   Were quite frightful to see,—
Till at last he put down a right bower,
   Which the same Nye had dealt unto me.

" Then I look'd up at Nye,
   And he gazed upon me ;
And he rose with a sigh,
   And said—' Can this be ?
We are ruined by Chinese cheap labour,'—
   And he went for that Heathen Chinee.

" In the scene that ensued
   I did not take a hand ;
But the floor it was strew'd
   Like the leaves on the strand,
With the cards that Ah-Sin had been hiding,
   In the game ' he did not understand.'

> "In his sleeves, which were long,
>   He had twenty-four packs,—
> Which was coming it strong,
>   Yet I state but the facts;
> And we found on his nails, which were taper,
>   What is frequent in tapers—that's wax.

> "Which is why I remark,
>   And my language is plain,
> That for ways that are dark,
>   And for tricks that are vain,
> The Heathen Chinee is peculiar:
>   Which the same I am free to maintain."

Though slight and incidental, there is no other lyric by BRET HARTE so perfect in form, so gently insidious in satire, so strong in conception, so firm in touch as this; just as there is no prose idyll so complete, pathetic, and direct in new emotional impact as the "Luck of Roaring Camp."

"Santa Claus" approaches it, "Miggles" is a formidable rival, and there is not a page of BRET HARTE which does not contain flashes of power, quaint turns and conceits of language, which can only come from a man who sees for himself with the eye of genius; and feels with the fresh heart of a little child; but he culminates unawares, and cannot repeat his successes.

No man, I should say, had his powers less at command, though apparently always able and ready to write, and write well.

No man shows so clearly when he writes about what he "knows," and when he writes about what he has "got up," when he writes to please himself, and when he writes to please others.

In the romance of Californian life; in the wild scenes of the New World; in the strange points of contact between the effete civilizations of Europe and the rough, raw material of new mining America; in those weird border lands of crime and heroism, where the dark spots in conventional virtue are used to set off the bright spots of habitual vice—there he is at home.

Whenever, as in the lengthy romance of "Gabriel Conroy," he attempts to mix up these elements with the general flow and routine of commercial, industrial, professional, and social life—clever, pains-taking, elaborate as is the performance, we lose the unique flavour.

BRET HARTE diluted almost ceases to be BRET HARTE ; he at once becomes California and water.

Give me the undiluted " Miggles," the unadulterated " Poker's Flat."

BRET HARTE has a gospel, in spite of his protest to the contrary.

He preaches it informally, but not the less effectually.

It is the old gospel of Belief in Human Nature which is to be found in the New Testament, and which has been forgotten by most modern theologians.

He preaches the virtue of the Publican, the purity of the Harlot, the lovableness of the Sinner.

The Author of the Christian religion, if I remember rightly, gave great offence by maintaining a somewhat similar paradox, when, turning to the self-satisfied and respectable people of the day, He remarked, " Verily I say unto you, that the Publicans and the Harlots go into the kingdom of God before you."

It seems that this truth is constantly in danger of being trampled upon, and that the human conscience is always infinitely grateful to any one who will reproclaim it boldly.

Yes! there is something in the nature of every man greater than himself—something which he needs must love even when he betrays it.

Nothing can quite drown the divine undertone : the light

in every man by which he must be saved is too well lit ever to be put out, however it may be blown in the winds of passion and dimmed in the fogs of vice.

As a moralist, when BRET HARTE has said that a man seeming to be bad is good—ay, better than he himself knows, or seeming to be good is bad, worse than he dreams, he has said all he has to say ; and of life generally, he would probably affirm, with COLERIDGE, that both good and bad men are less so than they seem.

But the value of BRET HARTE'S protest does not lie in the direction of " Lady Audley's Secret," as when he says, " The greatest scamp had a Raffaelle face, with a profusion of blonde hair," for, alas ! we are quite ready to believe that people may be less good than they appear ;—but rather in the divine secret, the secret of the Christian method as taught by the Master—that other belief, that people are less bad than they seem.

This faith it would appear impossible to keep to the fore. Yet this is so indispensable, that whenever it is stated lovingly, pathetically, and conscientiously the heart leaps up with gratitude and joy.

A thousand cobwebs are swept away.

We live in the delight and luxury of a recovered world.

We are no longer fastidious, even about the form.

Vulgarity, slang, impropriety, strangeness—everything in the narrative becomes accidental, unimportant.

The message is all in all.

The pearl of great price is found.

For this will a man surrender even all that he has ; he will buy the field with the rubble and the rock, so only he may get with it the hidden treasure.

So the " Luck of Roaring Camp " stood the fire of

criticism which raged against it both before and after its appearance.

The narrative turns on the way in which one touch of nature, one tender human instinct, is able to transform what is coarse and brutal and selfish into what is manly, decent, law-abiding, and even tender.

The helplessness of infancy checks the grossness of violence and greed.

The men are raised unconsciously and spontaneously by one genuine, unselfish human interest, external to themselves and to their grovelling pursuit of gold.

The little baby, the " Luck of Roaring Camp," offspring of Cherrokee Sal, a lost woman who dies and leaves this frail memory behind her, alone, unprotected, in the hands of these rough miners ; their care of it, their love for it, their unflagging and passionate interest in it ;—this is the deeply pathetic, often the deeply humorous, note of Roaring Camp.

How the profanity abates, how new thoughts and feelings are born, how the better life is called forth in the hearts of these coarse men and circles round the child like an aureole, it is needless here to relate.

The catastrophe is typical, and combines that high local colouring with a certain affecting choice of incident which gives such a charm to these Californian pictures :

" The winter of 1851 will long be remembered in the foot hills. The snow lay deep on the Sierras, and every mountain creek became a river, and every river a lake. Each gorge and gulch was transformed into a tumultuous water-course that descended the hill sides, tearing down giant trees and scattering its drift and *débris* along the plain. Red Dog had been twice under water, and Roaring Camp had been forewarned. ' Water put the gold into them gulches,' said Stumpy. ' It's been here once, and will be here again ! ' And that night the North Fork suddenly leaped over its banks and swept up the triangular valley of Roaring Camp.

"In the confusion of rushing water, crashing trees, and crackling timber, and the darkness which seemed to flow with the water and blot out the fair valley, but little could be done to collect the scattered camp. When the morning broke, the cabin of Stumpy, nearest the river-bank, was gone. Higher up the gulch they found the body of its unlucky owner; but the pride, the hope, the joy, the Luck of Roaring Camp had disappeared. They were returning with sad hearts when a shout from the bank recalled them.

"It was a relief boat from down the river. They had picked up, they said, a man and an infant, nearly exhausted, about two miles below. Did anybody know them, and did they belong here?

"It needed but a glance to show them Kentuck lying there, cruelly crushed and bruised, but still holding the Luck of Roaring Camp in his arms. As they bent over the strangely assorted pair, they saw that the child was cold and pulseless. 'He is dead,' said one. Kentuck opened his eyes. 'Dead?' he repeated feebly. 'Yes, my man; and you are dying too.' A smile lit the eyes of the expiring Kentuck. 'Dying!' he repeated; 'he's a taking me with him. Tell the boys I've got the Luck with me now;' and the strong man, clinging to the frail babe as a drowning man is said to cling to a straw, drifted away into the shadowy river that flows for ever to the unknown sea."

The "Luck of Roaring Camp" adds one more to the list of masterpieces that precisely on account of their excellence and novelty have been rejected or misunderstood.

We know that CHARLOTTE BRONTË had difficulty in finding a publisher for "Jane Eyre;" WASHINGTON IRVING'S "Sketch-book" had to be piloted by WALTER SCOTT; and even "Waverley" itself lay on the shelf for years.

The story of the "Luck," as given by BRET HARTE himself, is equally instructive and amusing.

It was, as he tells us, his first attempt to produce a distinctive Californian romance.

It was written for the *Overland Monthly,* of which he was the editor.

"I had not yet received the proof-sheets, when I was suddenly summoned to the office of the publisher, whom I found standing, the picture of dismay and anxiety, with the proof before him. My indignation and stupefaction can be well understood, when I was told that the printer, instead of returning the proofs to me, submitted them to the publisher, with the emphatic declaration that the matter thereof was so indecent, irreligious, and improper, that his proof-reader—a young lady—had with difficulty been induced to continue its perusal, and that he, as a friend of the publisher and a well-wisher of the magazine, was impelled to present to him personally this shameless evidence of the manner in which the editor was imperilling the future of that enterprise. It should be premised that the critic was a man of character and standing, the head of a large printing establishment, and, I think, a deacon. In which circumstances the publisher frankly admitted to me that, while he could not agree with all of the printer's criticisms, he thought the story open to grave objection, and its publication of doubtful expediency.

    *   *   *   *   *   *   *   *

Finally the story was submitted to three gentlemen of culture an 1 experience, friends of publisher and author, who were unable, however, to come to any clear decision."

As editor, he at last insists on the unpruned insertion of the " Luck," with what triumphant results all the world is well aware.

With that gentle tolerance and tender forbearance which reminds one of OLIVER WENDELL HOLMES'S own gracious and pardoning temper, he adds, with playful delicacy and a satire all his own :

" Across the chasm of years and distance the author stretches forth the hand of sympathy and forgiveness—not forgetting the gentle proof-reader, that chaste and unknown nymph whose mantling cheeks and downcast eye gave the first indication of warning."

In these few words on BRET HARTE, I have no desire to disparage his achievements as a good all-round literary man. He has written much and well. In his hands, the now fashionable " Roundabout Paper" has attained gigantic proportions.

There may be better novels than " Gabriel Conroy," with characters at once more devoloped and less laboured ; and THACKERAY'S prize novelists printed years ago in *Punch* will probably take higher rank than the " Condensed Novels " written for the *San Francisco California.*

When a man decides to reprint what the public will perhaps irreverently call his pot-boilers, it is often found that a good many of them are neither better nor worse than a good many essays written by several other people who possess no particular spark of genius.

A writer is finally judged not by the quantity, but by the quality of his work.

When all the excellent padding which serves its turn and passes out of the brain of this writer and out of the memory of his age, shall have had its little day and ceased to be, " Miggles " and the " Luck of Roaring Camp " will continue to be printed and read by delighted generations yet unborn, and the name of BRET HARTE will go down to posterity indissolubly wedded to that strange mood of civilization photographed in the " Outcasts of Poker's Flat," whilst American literature will be for ever enriched by the truth and tenderness of " Santa Claus."

EPILOGUE.

LADIES AND GENTLEMEN,

I have spoken my six pieces on the American Humorists.

I do not suppose, indeed I can hardly hope that you are as sorry to part with me as I am with you, for you are in the habit of listening to many more abstruse lecturers, but I have never addressed a more genial and appreciative audience.

My task has been sometimes a difficult and often a delicate one.

I trust you will acquit me of having ever been betrayed into mere levity or unbecoming frivolity. On the contrary, I have taken pains to vindicate the dignity and importance of the subject, by proving to you that Wit is not only the "best sense in the world," but that it is Moral, Recreative, and Stimulating in a very high degree.

I have shown that people who are not ashamed of Wrong are often afraid of Ridicule, and I have kept steadily before you, what I myself most firmly hold, that, wisely used and well, Wit is a most effective Disciplinarian, and one of the greatest sweeteners and purifiers of Life.

P

Milton Keynes UK
Ingram Content Group UK Ltd.
UKHW040929180224
437992UK00003B/115